# A PERFECT LIKENESS

◆ TWO NOVELLAS ◆

## RICHARD WAGAMESE

FOREWORD BY
WAUBGESHIG RICE

ORCA BOOK PUBLISHERS

Copyright © Richard Wagamese 2011, 2013, 2021
Foreword copyright © Waubgeshig Rice 2021

Published in Canada and the United States in 2021 by Orca Book Publishers.
*Him Standing* previously published in 2013 by Orca Book Publishers as a softcover
(ISBN 9781459801769) and as an ebook (ISBN 9781459801776, PDF; ISBN 9781459801783, EPUB).
*The Next Sure Thing* previously published in 2011 by Orca Book Publishers as a softcover
(ISBN 9781554699001) and as an ebook (ISBN 9781554699018, PDF; ISBN 9781554699025, EPUB).
orcabook.com

**Library and Archives Canada Cataloguing in Publication**
Title: A perfect likeness : two novellas / Richard Wagamese ; foreword by Waubgeshig Rice.
Other titles: Novellas. Selections
Names: Wagamese, Richard, author. | Rice, Waubgeshig, 1979- writer of foreword. |
Container of (work): Wagamese, Richard. Him standing. |
Container of (work): Wagamese, Richard. Next sure thing.
Identifiers: Canadiana (print) 20200299018 | Canadiana (ebook) 20200299026 |
ISBN 9781459828360 (softcover) | ISBN 9781459828377 (PDF) | ISBN 9781459828384 (EPUB)
Subjects: LCGFT: Novellas.
Classification: LCC PS8595.A363 A6 2021 | DDC c813/.54—dc23

Library of Congress Control Number: 2020942374

**Summary:** This volume contains two novellas by Richard Wagamese,
*Him Standing* and *The Next Sure Thing*. Both stories follow the lives
of young artists who have dreams for a better future.

Orca Book Publishers is committed to reducing the consumption of
nonrenewable resources in the making of our books. We make
every effort to use materials that support a sustainable future.

Orca Book Publishers gratefully acknowledges the support for its publishing
programs provided by the following agencies: the Government of Canada,
the Canada Council for the Arts and the Province of British Columbia
through the BC Arts Council and the Book Publishing Tax Credit.

Cover design by Dahlia Yuen
Cover image: Warrior mask by Ojibway carver Mathew Esquega
Author photo by Yvette Lehmann

Printed and bound in Canada.

24  23  22  21 • 1  2  3  4

# FOREWORD

IN ANISHINAABE CULTURE, WE ARE TAUGHT by our Elders to be kind and respectful. We are also told to carry ourselves with humility, and to put others before us whenever we can. There are many such teachings in our way of life, and we receive them through stories. Lessons and morals are passed down from generation to generation as stories are spoken and heard. Storytelling is a crucial practice that has kept culture alive in our communities, despite brutal measures by colonizing forces to erase it. In recent decades our courageous storytellers have brought us together in both healing and triumph as we continue on a path to understand our place as Indigenous people on this land.

Richard Wagamese was one of those iconic and important storytellers. He spoke his truth and shared his journey, overcoming the ravages of colonialism to bring people together and teach others. He emerged at a time when Indigenous voices were rarely heard or read in mainstream literature and journalism in Canada. Determined and spirited, he navigated his way through and around the white-dominated cultural institutions of this country to blaze a trail and tell his story and the stories of other Indigenous Peoples long silenced. He brought Indigenous experiences to the mainstream psyche at a time when the country was barely ready to learn about its true history. He helped usher in crucial awareness.

And Richard took all these pivotal steps guided by the Anishinaabe principles that were initially taken from him early in life. He was an intergenerational Survivor of the residential school system who, on top of that, survived the Sixties Scoop saga of child apprehension. He spent his adult life reconnecting with his family and community, and he candidly shared these experiences to encourage and inspire others to do the same. He was open about his own challenges and faults, which made his personal triumphs all the more empowering.

Richard succeeded at this because he was generous and humble. He knew the power of storytelling in all its forms, and how it could help his people heal and celebrate themselves. He wrote in a variety of voices and formats to reach as wide an audience as possible. He didn't want to leave anyone out of his storytelling circle, and this collection of two novellas is a sincere reflection of that. *The Next Sure Thing* and *Him Standing* are poignant stories about young Indigenous people navigating their way through urban life while staying true to their roots. And with his succinct, powerful telling of these stories, Richard once again found a way to help readers of all backgrounds connect.

While he provided an outlet and an opening for readers, he was just as passionate about helping aspiring Indigenous writers find their voice and place. He mentored me and many others over the course of his career, and for that I will always be thankful. I wouldn't be a published author today without his written words and his spoken guidance. I read his books as a youth and saw the potential for our stories and culture to thrive in the written word. When I started to write, he reached out and motivated me to be the best storyteller I could be. He remained an influential mentor and trusted friend of mine until his death.

He's gone now, but lives on through his work and the spirit of understanding he helped foster. And with stories and writings like these continually being reprinted and republished, wider audiences will benefit from his generosity and honesty. Richard wanted a better future for his people and everyone else who lives on this land. And we're getting there with each new reader of his stories.

—Waubgeshig Rice, Wasauksing First Nation

# HIM STANDING

# ONE

I GOT A TRICK WITH A KNIFE I LEARNED TO DO pretty good. It's not what you think. Despite all the crap about gangbangers and the gangbanger lifestyle, I got no part of that. No, the trick I do with a blade is that I make people. I can look at a perfect stranger for, like, maybe a minute, then turn around and carve his likeness into a hunk of wood. A perfect likeness. I've done it for lots of people. It's like I see them there. In the wood. Like they were there all the time. Like they were just waiting for me and my blade to come along and create them. It's a good trick.

Now, I ain't what you'd call established in a major way or

anything. But this talent, or whatever it is, got me a regular gig on the boardwalk. Thing is, I didn't even have to get a permit like the rest of the buskers and the charcoal sketchers. No, me, I lucked out. I chose the one guy out of a thousand, that summer day, who could help me. I sat him down and did him for free. I didn't know who he was at the time. Took me half an hour. Turned out the cat was with the city licensing department. When I finished, he said he was willing to give me the license in a straight swap for the carving. I'm no stooge. I took it. I been working the boardwalk ever since.

It's a pretty good nickel. Once your name gets out, people actually come looking for you. Lucas Smoke. Imagine that? Straight shootin', regular citizens calling my name. Seeking me out. Anyway, I started turning out, like, four of these a day for fifty bucks apiece. That's a two-hundred-dollar day, and that's nothing to sniff at. Beats freakin' workin', if you know what I mean.

Don't get me wrong. I never had anything against sweatin' and grindin' for a dollar if that's what a guy's gotta do. But there had to be options. It was my grandfather who turned me on to it. He was a carver. Did all these spooky faces he called spirit masks. They were big with the tourists. And then big with the galleries and collectors. Pretty soon my grandfather was rollin' in the dough. He was the only Ojibway on our reserve that had a house with three stories. Great big cedar-log house with floor-to-ceiling windows, overlooking the lake.

Then he handed me a knife one day and told me to make him in wood. I laughed. I was thirteen, and I had better things to do with knives. Like skinning a moose or filleting a fish. Something that had a purpose.

But he looked square at me the way grandfathers do and told me again to make him in wood. I don't know what happened. I know that I looked at him and I just saw him different. I saw angles and shadows and places where his face was irregular. I saw dips and planes and hollows. I started to carve. I had no idea what I was doing, but it was like my hands had a mind of their own. He said it was amazing. It was my grandfather who taught me everything I know about how to handle a blade. In fact, he gave me the knife. It's got a turtle-shell handle, and it's old. Really old. That's what he said. It was a traditional carver's knife. He said using it would connect me to the old-time magic of carvers. It's the knife I still use today.

That was seven years ago. My grandfather died when I was sixteen. Then the whole family started fighting over who got what. It made me sick. I missed the old man so much I ached all over. But all they could think about was the money, the house, the art and what it was worth. All I could think about was his hands. When he worked, they were a part of him but...not. That sounds crazy, but it was like they had their own spirit. They moved elegantly. That's a word he taught me. It means "energy set free." That's what he said. I could see that when he worked. And on a good day, I can see it in mine. Spirit moving in its own time.

So while the family squabbled, the whole thing ended up in court. And I booked it for the city. I didn't want any of my grandfather's things. I didn't want his money. I wanted him, and since I couldn't have him anymore, the reserve started to feel like some empty little backwater in the middle of nowhere. So I came to the city looking for any kind of job I could find. I was down to my last few bucks when I found the boardwalk.

Everywhere you looked, there were people doing weird and wonderful things. There were magicians, jugglers, a one-man band, contortionists and even a guy who drove nails into his head. They did it for the money and the applause. One day I sat on an empty bench and picked up a soft-looking piece of wood. I turned it over in my hands and started making a pretty woman in a hat who was looking out at the water a few yards away from me. Shavings were laid around my feet. There was a crowd gathered around me when I finished. The lady with the hat gave me thirty dollars. I did a couple more before the crowd drifted away. I came back to the rooming house where I live with almost a hundred bucks.

I met my girl on that boardwalk. Amy One Sky. She's a drop-dead gorgeous Ojib girl who works as a model and loves my work. She didn't even mind that I had next to nothing. She said I had a gift. She said she knew people who could get me my own show in a gallery. So I started working on pieces. Amy even got a few sold for me, and it looked like I was on the fast road to being a real artist.

Then Gareth Knight showed up on the boardwalk, and everything got weird real fast.

# TWO

IT WAS ONE OF THOSE PICTURE-POSTCARD
days. The sun was blazing, and the waves were roiling
in, all foamy and white against the blue. A slight breeze.
People everywhere. And the smell of hot dogs and candy
floss. It was a circus atmosphere. Everyone got turned
on by it. You could feel the energy all along the boardwalk. I did three pieces by two o'clock. There was a ring
of hangers-on around me constantly. I dug that action.
By this time Amy had put me in touch with people who
knew people, and my carvings were becoming known.
I had orders, for Pete's sake. But I still loved the feel of

the boardwalk. It was wild and outrageous. There were rock bands that plugged in and played. It put people in the mood to spend. To throw money in the hat I laid at my feet. I felt at home there.

There was this fat old guy who must have been in his seventies. He had a face built of wrinkles on top of wrinkles on top of at least three chins. He sat in the chair in front of me and asked me to do him. All I could think was that I didn't have a big enough piece of wood. But it was a fabulous face. There was so much detail to work with. His eyes sat behind globs of flesh and shone with a dark light, and his ears were clumps of meat. Fabulous. I was so captivated by it that all I could do was look at him.

"This magnificent face asks the best of you," I heard a voice say. "You aren't thrown off by a challenge, are you?"

I looked up from studying the fat guy's face. A man dressed all in black and leaning on a cane was looking straight at me. He had on an old-style fedora, the brim curled down over one eyebrow. A tiny sprout of beard grew just under his lower lip. His eyes were dark and glimmered in the light.

"I say you can't do it," he said. "In fact, this here says you can't."

He held up a roll of bills, and the crowd gasped. He smiled.

"I like a challenge," I said. "Let's see what I can do."

I picked up my biggest piece of pine and set it in my lap. The fat man splayed his feet apart and got comfortable in the chair. The sun cut deep shadows between his wrinkles. It would be hard. I looked up, and the man in black grinned at me and waved the roll of bills. I set to work.

Sometimes, when the work is good, I go way beyond time and space. I go somewhere else. I don't know where that place is, but I definitely lose contact with Earth. I exist in a separate world. A dream world, I guess, is the best way to describe it. Grandfather said that it is where stories are born. He said that when I carve, what I'm really doing is telling a story in wood. So the storytelling place is where I go when I'm really working well.

This time I was gone right away. I had no sense of time passing. I had no sense of concentration. I had no idea what people were doing around me. All I had was this fascination with my subject. The more I let myself feel that, the more

I felt myself slip away and become one with it. Corny? It used to seem that way to me. But I came out of that storytelling place the first time and held a finished piece in my hand that blew me away. I don't think it's corny anymore.

I don't know how long I was gone. I do know that it felt like my hands were on fire when I put the knife down. My breathing was ragged and I felt dizzy. But the crowd applauded when I set the likeness down on the small folding table I kept at my side. The fat man beamed with pleasure, mopped his face with a hankie and handed me fifty dollars. The carving was spectacular. I had caught every detail perfectly. The wood seemed to flow with the energy of that face.

The man in black nodded. He seemed pleased too. When he stepped forward and held out the roll of bills, the crowd around us clapped again. I stood up, took the money and reached out to shake the man's hand. It was cool, dry and taut with strength. He dipped his head and raised one hand to the brim of his hat in salute. A very gentlemanly move.

"An honor to watch you work," he said. "Gareth Knight is my name."

"Lucas Smoke," I said. "Thanks for this."

I waved the roll of bills. The one on the outside was a hundred, and I wondered if they all were.

"I know who you are," he said. "I've been watching the growth of your craft."

"Always nice to meet a fan."

"Not a fan, Mr. Smoke. More like an employer. I have a commission for you."

"Really? What did you have in mind?"

"A spirit mask. Like your grandfather did."

"You knew my grandfather?"

He offered a small smile.

"His work reached a great number of us."

"Us?"

"A circle of like-minded associates."

"I don't get it."

"You will. If you accept my offer."

"What exactly is this offer?"

"Ten times what's in your hand. Examine it when you get home. Call the number on my card."

He handed me a shiny black card with only his name and a telephone number on it.

"I don't do spirit masks," I said.

He smiled, and I suddenly felt very cold.

"You will," he said. Then he turned and disappeared into the crowd.

# THREE

THERE WERE FIFTEEN HUNDRED BUCKS IN THE roll. In hundreds and fifties. It was more money than I had ever seen in one place at one time. I held it in my hands and fanned it wide. I could feel an excitement I had never felt before start to glow in my belly. Amy watched me with a small smile on her face.

"You're like a little kid on Christmas," she said.

"Feels like it. I mean, ten times this will be more money than I've earned in my life," I said.

"Yes. But you have to earn it."

"What do you mean?"

"I mean you have to quit sniffing the advance and get to work, bucko."

We laughed. It felt good holding a wad of money and knowing there was more coming. All I had to do was get to work. But that bothered me. I still didn't know exactly what Gareth Knight wanted. I handed his card to Amy. She looked at it and rubbed her thumb across its slick surface.

"So this guy dressed all in black challenges you to carve a face. Then he hands you fifteen hundred bucks in a roll and offers you ten times that to do what your grandfather did?" she asked.

"Yeah, with a weird reference to a circle of like-minded associates."

"He sounds freaky," she said. "We should call him."

"Right now?"

"Why wait?" she asked. "I would never go on a shoot for someone I didn't know. Not unless I got full particulars."

"I suppose. Sure. Why not? Get the ball rolling here." I picked up the card and punched the numbers into the phone and held it to my ear.

Then a funny thing happened. We both heard the ring of the phone at the other end of the line. It rang just outside my door. At the same moment, there was a knock. I looked at Amy. She was as shocked as I was. I put the phone down and went to the door. I opened it to find Gareth Knight leaning on the jamb, waving his phone idly in his hand.

"You rang?" he asked and smiled.

"How did you know where I lived?" I asked.

He laughed. Then he straightened, adjusting his attire. He was still in black, but now he was dressed in jeans, boots, a T-shirt and a tuxedo jacket. A porkpie hat sat on his head at a rakish angle.

"I like to know where my money is going. I have associates who undertook to find that out for me. Nice accommodations, by the way. Very grungy in a struggling-artist sort of way. Nice aroma of cabbage, socks and grease."

He looked at Amy and bowed slightly.

"I'm a bit surprised to find you here, my dear."

"Well, I come with the territory," she said. "And besides, Mr. Knight, Lucas lives here because he wants to, not because he has to."

"I see. To soak up the atmosphere. Feed the muse, I suppose."

"Something like that," I said. The guy was starting to irritate me. "What are you doing here, anyway?"

"Same thing you were doing with the telephone, Lucas. Getting the ball rolling here."

Amy and I looked at each other in surprise. He had used the same words as me. He watched us with an amused expression.

"Now, may I come in to discuss details, or are you and Ms. One Sky going to keep me outside in this lovely hallway all day?"

"How do you know my name?" Amy asked. She sounded angry.

Knight touched the brim of his hat and nodded.

"Come now, Ms. One Sky. One needn't look far to find your face. And one needn't look far beyond that to find out who the face belongs to. A wonderful face, I might add. You should carve her, Lucas."

I stepped back to let him in. He strode by and inspected the room. It had never been much. Just a bed and a dresser, a small closet, an armchair and a table that held my carving tools and a few pieces of wood. He nodded, almost as if he liked it. Then he turned and regarded us with a raised eyebrow.

"Shall we discuss our arrangement?"

Amy and I sat on the bed, and Knight lowered himself slowly into the armchair. He looked at me calmly. I stared back at him for a long moment. Finally I cleared my throat.

"You're willing to pay me fifteen thousand for a spirit mask, even though you understand that I've never done a spirit mask. That's what it is, unless I missed something."

"Wonderfully summarized, Mr. Smoke."

"So what is it that you want exactly?"

"I want a legend brought to life."

"Excuse me?" I asked abruptly.

Knight grinned.

"I mean, I want the essence of a legend brought to life. As you do with all your work, Lucas. I want you to bring the spirit of a story forward."

"Which story is that?" I asked.

"That's where the work comes in, I'm afraid."

"Meaning?" Amy asked.

He looked at her and gave her a huge and dazzling smile. She blushed, and he smiled even harder.

"You have to dream," he said. "You have to allow yourself to inhabit the dream world. There you will find the legend and the story I want brought to life in wood. Your grandfather understood this way. It was the key to his work."

"He never shared that with me," I said.

"A pity. You'll have to learn it on your own then."

"How do I do that?"

"Sleep," he said, "perchance to dream."

"I've never dreamed very clearly," I said.

"You will."

"How can you be so sure?"

He leaned back in the chair and crossed one of his legs over the other. He made a steeple with his fingers and braced it under his chin.

"Because your grandfather left you his gift. It's rare, Lucas. Rare."

"Why should I believe that?"

"I can think of fifteen thousand reasons," he said and laughed.

# FOUR

NEITHER AMY NOR I WERE COMFORTABLE
once Knight had left. He was a mystery. We knew nothing
about him, except that he could throw around a lot of
money. While that was okay with me, I didn't like feeling
that I was on the outside of things. Dream? What was
that supposed to mean? My whole gig was built on carving
what I could see. If something was right in front of me, I
had no trouble making it appear in wood. But this? This
was just weird.

We spent the rest of the day trying to distract ourselves.
Amy led me to our favorite secondhand shops, the thrift

stores and flea markets where I bought all my clothes and stuff. Paying full price for things wasn't something I liked to do. Besides, things always felt better to me when I knew they had a life before I got them. I guess that's why I got so good at carving—I could feel history in things.

We ate at Amy's apartment. She's a good cook. She cut a steak into thin strips and stir-fried it with broccoli, snow peas, peppers, onions, mushrooms, tomatoes and spices that made it all tangy and hot. I loved it. Then we curled up on her couch and listened to music in the dark. That's one of the things we like the most. We turn off everything but the stereo and let the music flow over us in the darkness. It's really cool. You get right inside the music that way, and you hear things in it that you don't normally hear. We don't talk. We just listen. We spend hours that way.

After that I walked home.

Gareth Knight was still on my mind. I wanted to do the job. But there was something about it that bugged me. Knight never said anything straight. He just kind of laid something out there and expected you to run with it or let it hang. And talking about my grandfather—that bugged me a lot. The memory of my grandfather was so special that I never spoke of him. Even to Amy. All of us have things so precious we keep them to ourselves. Things we don't want to lose. Things we don't want changed from the way we remember them. I guess I didn't want anything to change about the way I remembered my grandfather. So I never spoke of him.

When I got home, I read for a while. I was actually afraid to sleep. I didn't think I bought the mumbo jumbo Knight had talked about. But it kept me awake. Legends brought to life? Legends were stories. Teaching stories. But they were just stories. There weren't real people in them. They were all dream people.

I tossed and turned once I shut the light off. I thought about getting up and working on something. Instead, I just lay there. Finally, after an hour or so, I drifted off.

I found myself on a riverbank in the moonlight. It was made of stones. There was a tall cliff behind me and a narrow path twisting its way upward. Across the river was another cliff, but this one was less steep. There was a thick carpet of trees on its face. The moon hung right over the middle of the water. The river had eased out of a long, sweeping turn, and the current was slow. It was summer, and the night was cool but not uncomfortable.

There was a canoe on the beach a few yards away from me. I suddenly wanted to paddle. I walked over and pushed the canoe into the water. I waded in knee-deep and stepped over the gunwale and into the canoe. I began to paddle. I could see the reflection of the moon on the calm water. A light breeze barely disturbed the peaceful night air.

But suddenly the wind rose. It came blustering out of the upstream sweep of the river and quickly turned the water to chop. The canoe begin to buck in the waves. The current grew stronger. The canoe was pushed downstream. Nothing I could do would change its course. The river churned and the canoe dipped crazily. I heard laughter. I looked around, but there was no one there. The laughter boomed out across the water.

Then I heard the thunder of a waterfall. I could see the spume rising in clouds a half mile ahead of me. The roar of it grew louder. There was nothing I could do to stop the canoe. The laughter rumbled off the cliffs all around me.

I flailed at the water with the paddle. The canoe hurtled forward. I felt my insides turn to water. Just as it reached the edge of the waterfall, I looked up. There was the face of a man in the moon. He was laughing. That's all I saw before the bow dropped and the canoe plummeted. I hit the pool at the foot of the falls and was pushed down deeper and deeper, as if by a giant hand. The frigid water produced a burning sensation.

I spun in the crazy current. I had no idea which way was up. Then I heard a voice say, "Open your eyes." That's all. It was a deep bass voice. Commanding. I opened my eyes. All I could see was eerie, dark blue. Then I saw the moon. I kicked hard toward it. As I got closer to the surface, the image became clearer. Then I saw the face. A shaman's face, painted black with three wavy red lines running down its right cheek. Looking down at me from the face of the moon.

"Do you see me?" the voice asked.

I clawed frantically for the surface. "Yes," I said.

"Bring me to life," it said.

"I can't," I said.

"Then die."

I felt icy hands push me deeper into the pool. My lungs wanted to explode. The moon had vanished. There was only the terrible dark of the water.

I woke up bathed in a cold sweat.

# FIVE

AT FIRST, IT WAS ONLY DREAMS. THEY SEEMED to come even before I was fully asleep. All I had to do was close my eyes, and I was deep in the shimmer of light and color. Each of them was a story. Each of them had something to do with the shaman. I was in them as an observer. But I could see everything. I knew the man had power. I knew that he was a wizard, a sorcerer. I knew that he had lived a long time ago, before white people came to North America. I knew that he was cold. Heartless. I knew that he was mean.

But they were such grand dreams. I saw parts of the life my people had led many years ago. I saw trappers and hunters. I saw canoe makers, drum builders, toolmakers, hide tanners and men who were born to fight. Everywhere I looked in those dreams, I felt as though I was there. It was like they were shining a light on my own history, and I found myself eager to go to them, to find myself in them, to be among those people.

Those people included the man with the painted face. He carried a powerful magic. He lived alone, apart from the people, and when the smoke rose from his wigwam, the people seemed to creep around their camp. Songs and drumming and strange incantations came from that lodge then. Sometimes it would shake as though there was a violent struggle going on inside. The people averted their eyes. No one spoke. Everyone was afraid. But I couldn't take my eyes off that small wigwam in the trees.

Amy began to notice a change in me.

"You're so quiet lately," she said. "Is everything all right?"

"It's fine," I said. I was scraping a bevel-edged chisel along a line of wood and didn't look at her.

"It doesn't feel fine, Lucas. You feel far away from me."

"I'm busy," I said.

"You're always busy lately. But I never see anything get done. You stare off into space and rub the edge of a tool on wood, but you don't create anything."

I stood up suddenly. I could feel the raw, dark edge of anger in my gut.

"Are you going to start telling me how to work?" I asked. It didn't feel like my voice.

She sat back farther in her chair. She looked at me wide-eyed.

"You never raised your voice at me before," she said quietly.

I felt guilty. The anger had risen in me before I knew it was even there.

"I'm sorry," I said in my own voice. "This whole project has got me anxious, and I was never anxious about a piece before."

"It's the money, isn't it?"

"Yeah. That and Knight and the damn dreams."

"What dreams?"

I looked out the window at the skyline of the city. I spoke without looking at her. I told her about the vision of the camp and how it almost felt like I'd been transported back in time. How real the people and their lives seemed. I told her about the man with the painted face. I left out the part about the wigwam shaking and the feeling of blackness that fell over everything when that happened. I told her everything except the hold these dreams were starting to have on me. Like I needed them. Like I couldn't wait to get back to them.

"Knight told you to dream," she said. "He said you would."

"I haven't seen the legend though," I said.

"Maybe the legend is in the lives of the people."

"Too ordinary," I said. "Knight's after something heavy."

"Heavy as in what?" she asked.

I spun in my seat so fast, it shocked both of us. I stood up. Suddenly I felt heavier, bulkier, taut with muscle. My face felt like a chunk of stone. It was a heady feeling. I felt incredibly powerful. The voice that came out of me was harsh and sharp like a hiss.

"There are powers and secrets best not spoken, girl child."

Amy stood up and backed away from me. Her hand was at her throat, and her eyes were huge and scared-looking.

I took a step toward her. She held the other hand out to keep me at arm's length.

"Don't," she said.

"Amy, I…I…" I stuttered.

"Just don't, Lucas. Don't do or say anything."

I felt smaller then, back to my usual size. My body sagged. There was a feeling in my head like the moment after an accident happens and you wonder where you are. I still had the chisel in my hand. I looked at it dumbly and laid it on the table. She was watching me closely. When I slumped into my chair, I saw her slowly start to relax.

"You called me girl child, Lucas. You never speak like that."

"Sorry," I mumbled.

"And your face? Your face was wild. Your eyes were almost red. I thought you were going to attack me with the chisel."

"I wouldn't," I said.

"*You* wouldn't, no."

"What's that supposed to mean?"

"I mean, I've never seen you react like that. It's like you were someone else. Someone I don't want to know."

I stared at the floor. I felt as though a chunk of time had been ripped from my life. It was as though I'd been pushed to the sidelines and forced to watch as things went on. As though I had no power to step off those sidelines and say or do anything different. But I couldn't tell her that. It made no sense to me. If it made no sense to me, it was sure not going to make any sense to her. I felt sure of that.

"I'm just stressed," I said. "I'll get some better sleep tonight and I'll be fine."

"This work isn't good for you. It scares me. You scare me."

All I could do was look at her and nod.

# SIX

ONE MORNING MY HANDS TOOK ON A LIFE OF their own. I'd found a nice piece of cedar that was large enough for a life-size mask. I split it with a tree-felling wedge and a small sledgehammer. I had to be careful. I wanted a perfect half round to work with. I needed the grain in the wood to be consistent and clear. I carefully chiseled the bark off. I moved slowly. I tapped the end of the chisel lightly, then guided it forward with my hands so the bark would come off easily. It took some time, but I ended up with a glistening, reddish surface with a fine grain. I'd never done this before. But somehow I knew how.

That didn't bother me. What bothered me was how I suddenly was able to just carve at will. Normally there was a subject, someone I could look at, that made the magic happen. But now there was nothing. There was only the recollection of the dreams. There was only the painted face. I tried to go through the specifics of the dreams. I wanted to figure out which legend Gareth Knight wanted me to carve. But all I could see was the dim painted face of the man in the wigwam. That's when my hands began to really move on their own.

I hadn't had a clear look at him since the first dream of the waterfall. Even that wasn't detailed enough. The face was flat. It had no edges or angles or hollows, and I didn't know what the bone structure was. All I saw was the leering, painted face. But my hands knew what to do. I sat there for hours every morning. It was like I fell into a spell. Time just disappeared. I don't know what happened to me during those times. But I do know that by the time I came out of them, there were shavings all around my feet. And I felt thick. Like my blood was sludge. Like my head was stuffed with cotton. Opening my eyes was like coming out of a coma. It was like I had left the world behind me. I felt odd, out of shape, not comfortable in my own body.

Every morning I would wake and sit with my coffee, looking out my window over the neighborhood. Every morning I would try to get a fix on the face. It wasn't a legend, but it was the one thing that kept coming to me. I couldn't shake it. I was worried Knight would call off the deal. I wanted that money. I wanted it bad.

Then I would move to my work table, and the day would disappear.

One day, after about a week of this, the telephone rang. I didn't answer it. I couldn't. Nothing existed for me but the mask, the face. I couldn't take my eyes from the work I was doing. It rang again. I let it ring. It rang three times before I could break out of the trance I was in to pick it up. Finally I picked it up.

"Yes?" The word came out of me dully.

"Is that you, Lucas?"

"Yes." It was the same thick voice.

"Lucas?" It was Amy. "Are you all right? You sound different."

"Yes," I said again. It seemed to be all I could say.

"Lucas, you're scaring me. I haven't seen you in nearly a week. You don't call. You don't answer voice messages, and you sound like you're stoned."

"Yes," I said.

"I'm coming over there right now."

I lay the phone in its cradle and stared at the wall.

I was still doing that when Amy walked into the apartment. I turned slowly to look at her. She shrank back against the door.

"Oh my god," she said. "Lucas."

"What?" I asked. I tried to smile, but the muscles in my face felt odd.

She walked toward me slowly. Her eyes were wide. "Your face," was all she said.

"What about my face?" My mind was clearing now that she was here.

"It's different."

"Different how?"

"It's older. It's definitely older."

"Can't be," I said, coming back to myself. "It's only been a few days."

She looked around the room. Except for the mess on

my work table, the place looked tidy. When she came to sit across from me, there was a worried look in her eyes.

"You haven't been eating," she said. "There're no dirty dishes and your garbage is the same as the last time I saw it."

"No time," I said. "All I've been doing is working. Sleeping. Dreaming. Working."

"Dreaming about what, Lucas?"

"Don't know. Can't find the legend. Only got a face."

"What face?"

"The painted man. That's all I got. Painted man's face."

"Can you show me what you've done so far?"

I got up sluggishly. My body felt that same odd heaviness, and I couldn't get my feet to move. Finally I summoned enough strength to walk slowly over to the work table. The mask was covered with a black cloth. I didn't know where the cloth had come from. We stood side by side looking at it, and I could feel Amy's worry.

"That's it," I said. "The mask. The mask of the painted man's face."

"Is it finished?" Amy asked.

"No," I said. "It seems to be taking a really long time."

"Have you heard from Gareth Knight?"

"No. But he'll be pleased that I'm working."

"Even if it's going as hard and slow as you say?"

"Yes." I said it in the dreamy, detached voice she had heard on the phone.

She looked at me. Then she reached out and slowly pulled the black cloth from the carving. I heard her moan. I heard a sob in her throat. She looked at me with eyes brimming with tears.

"Lucas," she said shakily.

When I looked at the carving, I was staring at a blurred outline of my own face.

# SEVEN

I SAT THERE IN DISBELIEF. I'D WORKED SO hard. It felt like the hardest work I had ever done. Now, there was just my face. I thought I was carving the painted man. I thought I was entering the dreams and coming out with a better idea of how to bring him to life in the wood. Amy and I sat there not knowing what to say. I felt beaten. I felt terrified. The week had been one long blur, and this was all I had to show for it. Amy looked scared. Plumb scared. She put both hands to her face and stared without blinking at the mask.

"I don't understand," she said quietly.

"Me neither," I said.

"I don't think you should do this anymore."

"I can't stop now."

"Why? It's not good for you, Lucas."

"There's too much on the line," I said.

"It's just money. You're a talented artist. You'll get more work. This is just weird, and it's not affecting you in a good way." She reached out and touched me lightly on the arm.

What happened next shocked both of us. I pushed her arm away with a sweeping motion and reached out and grabbed her by the shoulders. I stared hard into her eyes. The muscles in my face tightened so hard, I thought they would snap. I scowled. I shook her hard. There was a cold hardness in my chest. I was shaking. The voice that came out of me wasn't mine.

"The doorway is open. It will stay open, girl child. When I emerge, you will see real power!"

Amy scrambled out of my grip. She backed into the corner and stared wide-eyed at me. When I took a step, she held both hands out in front of her to ward me off. My feet were heavy, bulky. My arms and shoulders were tight. The scowl was still on my face. I put my hands up to my face and clutched both temples. I was terrified and sick and suddenly very weak. Before I knew what was happening, I had collapsed onto my knees in the middle of the room and was shaking violently.

"What's happening to me?" I howled.

"Not exactly feeling like yourself, Lucas?" I looked up. Gareth Knight stood in the doorway. We hadn't heard the door open. He was still dressed in black. The room felt colder all of a sudden. Amy strode over to kneel beside me. "The work is proceeding well, I see," Knight said.

Amy put her arms around me, and we watched as Knight stepped over to my work table. He laid a hand on his chin as he studied the mask. There was a small grin at the corners of his mouth, and he nodded.

"Very good," he said. "The spirit is growing stronger. Any interesting dreams lately, Lucas?"

"He's not going to do your work anymore," Amy said, standing up to face Knight. "You can keep your commission."

Knight smiled.

"Very bold, Ms. One Sky," he said. "I think I like that. But you see, Lucas and I have a gentleman's agreement. Don't we, Lucas?"

He tilted his head a little and looked at me. His eyes seemed to swim. They were like black seas. I felt I was being swept up in their tide.

"Yes," I said dully.

"You see, Ms. One Sky? He understands the nature of our deal. And besides, you really want to see this through, don't you, Lucas?"

"Yes," I said again. The word slid from my mouth with a hollow sound.

"Not a very wordy reply, but you can see he wants to do the job," Knight said. "It's not a good idea to cross an artist when he wants to create. It's not good to get between them and their work."

"He doesn't know what he's saying," Amy said. "Can't you see that?"

"Oh, I think Lucas knows exactly what he's saying. Don't you, Lucas?"

I looked at him. I stared into his eyes. Now they were glittering. I couldn't look away. I felt pulled deeper into them. My head felt cloudy, dreamy. I held his look and stood up slowly. When I did, I felt the odd heaviness in my body, and the room seemed suddenly smaller.

"The doorway is open," I said, and I heard Amy gasp.

Knight smiled again and broke the look.

"Yes. The doorway is open. You want to keep it open, don't you? And you won't let Ms. One Sky talk you out of it, will you?"

"The doorway will remain open. It will be finished. The girl child will not stop it." The voice was cold and stern. Amy stepped away from me.

"Who are you?" she asked Knight. "Where did you come from?"

"I'm just a simple art lover, my dear," Knight said. "As to where I came from, well, where do we all come from, Amy child? Are we not the same?"

"We're not the same," she said. "We don't walk around scaring people for the thrill of it. And I'm not a child."

"No. You're not. You're an adult. Just like Lucas is an adult. Free to make choices, free to decide what he wants and what is good for him."

"You've got him under some kind of spell or something," Amy said.

Knight laughed. It was a wild, rollicking laugh. But his eyes showed no humor. They were cold and flat and hard.

He crossed one leg behind the other and leaned on the cane he carried.

"There is no spell. There is only desire. Your desire is to finish the mask, isn't it, Lucas?"

"Yes," I said dreamily.

He nodded. Amy looked at me and I felt my head clear. When we looked at the doorway, Knight had vanished.

# EIGHT

"I'M SO WORRIED," AMY SAID.

Soon after Knight left, my head had begun to clear.
I recalled everything that had happened, but I could make no
sense of it. It felt as though I had only been an onlooker. Now,
sitting at the table sipping tea with Amy, I was worried too.

"It's like I can't do or say anything when that guy's
around," I said.

"We need to find a way to get you out of this," Amy
said.

"I don't think there's a way. The guy scares me actually.
I kinda think he's a half step away from crazy."

"I think he's already there. But I think what we need to do is get out of here for a while. You need groceries anyway. Let's do the market thing."

"Good idea," I said.

I was starting to feel back to myself, glad for her company and eager for some regular routine. Going to the market was one of our favorite things. We always rode our bikes. We got to pedal through our favorite parts of the city, and both of us enjoyed the trips. I was more than ready for an outing.

"Let's do it. We can get some of those muffins you like."

She smiled, but there was still a grave look in her eyes.

The day was brilliant with sunshine. There was only a hint of a breeze, and the sidewalks were filled with shoppers and people busy with their lives. It felt good to be out among them. We stuck to the bike lane and pedaled slowly, side by side. I took in the sights that I never seemed to grow tired of. When you're down to your last dime like I had once been, you get to like simple things. When your butt is on the sidewalk, even simple things seem a thousand miles away from you. Riding a bike and seeing so much activity was a pure pleasure.

The market was in one of those cool areas where there were bookstores, cafés, art shops, clothing boutiques and music stores. The people were mostly young, and there was a nice energy. No one ever looked twice at you, so you could just settle, feel relaxed and go about your business. That's why I liked going there. We found a rack to lock our bikes in and walked hand in hand to the market.

Amy had turned me on to really good food. I was just a regular Kraft Dinner and tuna kind of guy before I met her. A can of beans and wieners was a big night for me. But Amy knew about all these different sorts of veggies and fruits, crackers, cheeses, soups and things I never would have imagined in a million years. So shopping with her was like exploring. I never knew what we'd come out with.

We separated, and I took my time browsing the aisles. I liked the language of food. There were all kinds of cool words, like *wasabi, cannelloni* and *gourd*. I liked the way they felt on my tongue. One of my favorite things was to grab a can or a box and repeat the words on the label to myself. I was doing that when I saw a tiny lady down the aisle, trying to reach something on the top shelf. She couldn't get at it.

She looked to be about eighty. She had big cheekbones, dark eyes, brown skin and long white hair tied back under a kerchief like the one my grandmother wore. She was obviously Native. I put the box I was holding back on the shelf and walked over to her.

"Let me help you," I said.

She looked at me kindly. Then, as I got close, her expression changed. She looked scared. She started backing away from me quickly, with her hands up in front of her.

"No!" she said. "Get away!"

I looked behind me. I couldn't believe she was shouting at me.

"Lady," I said, "chill out. I'm just trying to help you."

"I didn't invite you," she said. "You are not welcome here!"

She backed away faster, and when she tried to turn, her feet slipped out from beneath her. I hurried toward her. She scrambled to her feet and began trotting toward the exit. I couldn't understand why she was so scared. I wanted to show her that I wasn't a threat. Plus, I didn't want any heat from security or the cops. So I followed her.

She tried to round a corner and ran straight into

another old lady's shopping cart and tipped it over. Amy came out of the next aisle to see what the noise was all about. She saw me approach the old lady, who was scrambling amid the cans and boxes and trying to get to her feet.

"Ma'am," I said, "it's all right. I'm only trying to help you."

"You're not welcome here," she said again. "Go back where you came from."

Amy looked at me curiously. The manager came hotfooting over and bent to help the woman to her feet. But his feet slipped in some spilled milk, and he tumbled down beside her. Amy went to the woman and knelt beside her.

"What is it?" Amy asked. "What can I do to help you?"

The old lady clutched Amy's arm. Hard. She pointed at me.

"Him Standing," she said shakily, almost in tears. "Him Standing."

"What?" I said. "Me?"

"You are not welcome. I did not invite you," the woman said.

Amy helped her to her feet. The woman just stood there for a moment. Then she grabbed Amy by the elbows and looked into her eyes.

"The shaman has returned," she said.

"What shaman?" Amy asked.

The woman pointed a shaking finger at me.

"There," she said.

"That's my boyfriend," Amy said quietly. "That's Lucas."

"No," the old lady said. "No!"

She broke Amy's grip and again made for the exit. We looked at each other. When we tried to go after her, the manager and a security guard blocked our way.

"Sir," the security guard said, "you're going to have to come with me."

# NINE

I EXPLAINED WHAT HAD HAPPENED AS BEST
I could. After checking the tapes from the security cameras
and seeing that I had never touched the old woman in any
way, they let me go. There was nothing they could hold me
for. Amy was waiting outside the security office. When she
saw me, she ran up and gave me a big hug.

"Lucas," she said, "what was that? Why was that woman
so terrified of you?"

"I don't know," I said. "What was it she called me?"

"It was odd. A name, I think."

"Him Standing," I said. "*The shaman has returned.*"

"Yes. That's what she said."

"What does it mean?"

"I have no idea. It was weird though. Really, really weird."

"Got that right."

We walked past the mess in the aisle. The janitor was sweeping up the dry goods. His partner had a mop and was sopping up the spills. I shook my head at the weirdness of it all. Amy grabbed my arm and stopped me in my tracks.

"Lucas," she said, "what's that?"

She pointed to something lying just under the edge of the shelving. It looked to be a small feather. I got on my hands and knees and slid it out. I picked it up and handed it to Amy. It was a small brown feather with speckled bits of brown and white at its bottom end. The spine was decorated with three tiny beads and a loop of leather thong. The beads were wonderful.

"What are they?" I asked.

Amy studied them awhile and rubbed them with the nub of a finger.

"Glass," she said. "They look handmade."

"People make handmade glass?"

"Artists do. They use a torch to melt glass together to make beads."

"What do you mean?"

"Look at the beads. Do you see how they have all kinds of different swirls of color in them?"

"Yeah. So?"

"So," she said with a smile, "a glass artist heats glass into a blob with a metal rod through the middle. Then they turn it so it gets round. Then they melt other colors of glass into the original blob and create unique kinds of beads. That's what this is."

"You know a lot about this," I said, impressed.

"I have a lot of jewelry that's made out of glass. I read up about how they make it."

"So you think the old lady made this?"

"Yeah," she said. "Maybe. Or she bought it from someone who works with feathers and Indian kinds of materials."

"It's nice," I said. "We should get it back to her."

"And maybe we could ask her what she meant by all that shaman stuff," Amy said. "I don't know what she meant by *you are not invited* either. It was weird."

We rode our bikes over to Amy's place. She lived in a nice condo in a cool, light pink building. The color reminded me of a drink they serve with tiny umbrellas sticking out of it. It was a nice place. I liked going there. Her place had floor-to-ceiling windows that let in a lot of light, and it just felt good in there. Amy also had a lot of nice furniture and a kick-ass stereo system. She got me to listen to music I'd never heard before. I liked doing that. She knew I was embarrassed because I was poor, but she always took care to make me feel comfortable. I never felt out of place there. But I still preferred to sleep in my room.

She had a computer too. After we'd eaten and had some coffee, we went into her den to search online for places where glass beads were made and sold. It was odd, but with all the light in Amy's place, I didn't feel any of the strange things I'd felt working on the mask. She was a whiz on the computer, and it didn't take her long.

"Look, Lucas," she said, holding a finger to the screen.

I leaned in and read.

"Sally Whitebird. Fused glass from a Native perspective."

"She would know where this came from," Amy said. "And it's only a short walk away. Wanna check it out?"

"Sure," I said. "It'd be good to get a handle on this weirdness."

Amy smiled. "Nice to have you back," she said.

I kissed her. I felt safe. I felt like myself. Amy was good medicine.

We walked out of her building and headed into the neighborhood where Sally Whitebird's glass studio was. Whitebird. It sounded like an Ojibway name, but I had never met anyone called that. I wondered if she knew anything about some shaman called Him Standing, and why someone might confuse me with him. I wondered if she knew why the woman in the market would be so scared.

We found the place easily. It was small, like a cottage. There were a lot of trees and bushes in the yard, and flowers and ferns everywhere too. It looked peaceful.

Amy rang the bell and we waited. We could hear a drum and chanting. The sounds stopped, and there was a moment of silence before we heard footsteps. I took the beaded feather out of my jacket pocket and held it in front of my chest. We heard the rattle of several dead bolts, and the door opened a crack. We saw a brown eye. Then we heard a groan. Then a cry. Then the sound of a body falling to the floor.

I tried to push the door open, but the body was blocking it. I pushed harder and got it open just enough for Amy to slide between the jamb and the door. I heard her rustling around. Then the door opened and there she stood, with the body of a woman lying on the floor behind her.

"My god," she said. "It's the woman from the market, Lucas. *She's* Sally Whitebird."

# TEN

SHE MUST HAVE GIVEN HERSELF A GOOD conk on the noggin, because she didn't move at all when I moved her to her couch. She was tiny. She felt like air in my hands. Amy arranged pillows behind her head. I found the kitchen and returned with a glass of water and a cold cloth. The old lady still hadn't stirred.

Her home was what some people would call exotic. All the furniture was made of wood. There was no glass or chrome anywhere, except for mirrors. The carpets were the old-fashioned rag kind. The kind old ladies like my grandmother used to make. The only flowers were dried, and there were tree branches in the corners of the room. The branches were hung with feathers and beads like the ones we'd found. There were a couple of stuffed birds and a hornet's nest on a shelf. On the wall above a small fireplace was a bear hide. A large seashell decorated a coffee table that looked like a section of tree trunk.

"Interesting," I said.

Amy looked up from mopping the woman's brow with the cloth and scanned the room.

"She really likes to keep nature close," she said.

"Wonder what the rest of the joint looks like?" I said.

"Probably a lot like this room," Amy said. "She seems like a very rustic person."

The woman groaned. Amy laid the cloth on her forehead and took her hand. I saw the old woman squeeze it. I could see the blue of her veins through her light-brown skin. Her skin was papery and brittle-looking. Slowly she came back to herself. Her eyes fluttered and then opened, and she looked at Amy.

"You found me," she said.

"Yes," Amy said. "It wasn't hard. The Internet and all."

"A whole other kind of magic," she said, and then she

looked over at me. She didn't panic. Instead, she gazed at me steadily. "I'm Sally Whitebird."

"Amy One Sky. And this is Lucas Smoke. He's my boyfriend, like I told you at the market."

"He did not follow you here," she said.

"Who?" I asked.

"Him Standing," she said. "Or his agent." Amy held the water glass to Sally Whitebird's mouth, and she took a small sip. Then she lay back against the pillows and closed her eyes. Amy looked at me with a worried expression. I whirled one finger around my ear, and she frowned at me.

"You were really scared at the market," Amy said. "You thought Lucas was someone else."

Sally groaned and put her forearm over her eyes. She breathed deeply and steadily for a few moments.

"He was there. I saw him in your face." She turned to me and looked at me with clear, dark eyes. "His shadow was all around you."

"But he's not here right now?" I asked.

"No. You've been to a place of light."

"What does that mean?" Amy asked.

"The dark shamans do not like light. It robs them of their energy."

"We were at Amy's," I said.

"A place of light?" she asked and blinked.

"Yeah," I said. "It always has been for me. I like it there. Different from where I live."

"He cannot venture there. It is a strong place. Like here. Dark medicine cannot enter here. There is too much shining, good energy."

"That's why you're not afraid of me now?" I asked.

"Yes," she replied. "I was scared at the door. But not now. Now I see that things have come to their proper place."

"We don't understand any of this," Amy said. "Our lives have actually been really strange this last little while."

"He is trying to return," Sally said. "He has been gone for generations, and I once thought that no one knew of him anymore, that he existed only as a legend."

"Bring a legend to life," I said.

"What?" Sally asked. She struggled to sit upright, and Amy reached out to help her. She was so small, her feet barely reached the floor.

I told her about Gareth Knight. I told her about his

challenge on the boardwalk and about the big lump of money he gave me. She listened intently. So I told her about my grandfather, and how he'd passed his carving skills on to me. I told her about the trick with the knife that I could do. Then I told her about Knight's directions for me to dream and carve a spirit mask to bring a legend back to life.

"Only I never saw a legend. I only ever saw the face. A painted face."

"Black. With three wavy red lines down one side. The right side," Sally whispered.

"Yes. Does that mean something?"

"It is not the heart side," Sally said. "It means he does not feel like we do. His emotions are blocked. He is a weaver of dark magic."

"And Gareth Knight?" Amy asked. "How does he fit into this?"

"A man dressed in black is the agent of the dark shaman. He is a summoner, a follower of Him Standing's medicine way. He is a shaman himself but without the great power of Him Standing. He wants the spirit of the dark shaman to inhabit the mask so he can wear it and assume that power."

"How did he find his way to me?" I asked.

Sally crossed the room and picked up a rattle made from a turtle shell. She shook it in a wide circle. It sounded old and powerful.

"Your grandfather knew these things. He put legends into spirit masks. When he taught you, that energy was transferred to you."

"But he never told me anything about any of this. He only taught me to carve," I said.

"That is the weakness they take advantage of," Sally said and shook the rattle again. "Those who know the how of things but not the why. They know how to do things but not the spiritual reason they do them."

"What do we do then?" I asked.

She looked at me with iron eyes.

"We fight," she said.

# ELEVEN

THE WAY SALLY TOLD THE STORY, IT SEEMED like a movie she'd seen. Him Standing was a member of a dark-medicine society. They were wizards. Sorcerers. They were at war with the shamans of light. The good-medicine people. The dark shamans wanted to control people, make them do their bidding. To make themselves more powerful. The shamans of light worked with the people to make them stronger. To guide them in spiritual ways that would keep them safe and strong. They were a threat to the wizards. As long as they were around to make people stronger, the dark medicine had less power.

So the dark shamans created powerful magic that robbed people of their power. They were scary. They were heartless. They were the reason behind wars. Their power was in the fear they created.

Him Standing was the most powerful of the dark shamans. He had been raised with good-medicine people. But a dark master offered him riches and power. He was only a boy and was easily swayed. He became the dark master's student, and he learned quickly. By the time he was a young man, Him Standing was feared far and wide. Sally said it was because he understood both kinds of medicine and combined them to build his power. All he had to do was stand at the edge of a village, and the people fell under his control. A lot of good-medicine people died fighting him.

But a wise shaman named Otter Tail found a way to beat him. One winter he challenged Him Standing to a race. They would race across a frozen lake. The first to make it across and back would win the right to work with the people of the village, who stood on the shore to watch. Him Standing laughed. The good shaman was small. There was no way he could match the wizard's strength and speed.

At first, Him Standing was far ahead. Otter Tail only walked. When he got to the far side, the dark shaman roared with laughter. It echoed off the hills. The people were scared. He began to run in big thumping bounds back across the lake. He followed his own tracks through the snow.

But he was heavy. The first crossing had weakened the ice. The second time he crossed the lake, the ice broke. Him Standing fell into the freezing water. His anger was huge. His strength was enormous. He swung at the edge of the ice to try to get a grip. But his anger only broke more of it off.

He tried to use his magic to call fish to swim under him and lift him up. But the cold weakened him. No fish came to his rescue. He was drowning.

Otter Tail stood yards away from the hole in the ice.

"You must help me!" Him Standing said.

"Why?" Otter Tail asked.

"Because you are good," Him Standing gasped.

"You were good once."

"I know. I am sorry. I will change."

"How do I know this is true?" Otter Tail asked.

"I give my word," Him Standing said. "Please."

"Let us make a trade then," Otter Tail said.

"Yes. Anything."

"I will trade you worlds. I will spare you, but you must reside forever in the dream world."

"If I do not agree?" Him Standing asked. His teeth were chattering. His grip on the ice was loosening.

"Then die and have no world," Otter Tail said.

Him Standing bobbed under. He flailed in the water. He got a grip on the edge of the ice again. His head was barely above the surface.

"Yes. All right. I will take your deal."

With that, Otter Tail took a turtle-shell rattle from his robes. He shook it in a wide circle around Him Standing. He spoke in words they didn't understand. The people on the shore watched in amazement as the wizard was lifted from the water. He spun rapidly in the air. Then he vanished.

Sally paused and looked at me steadily. "He went to the dream world. He has lived there ever since. His followers have tried to bring him back many times. But they needed a source of pure magic."

"Me?" I asked.

"Yes," Sally said. "Your grandfather shared his gift with you. But you had it in you already. That is why you create so easily. That is why you do what you do without study. It is pure magic."

"Gareth Knight saw that on the boardwalk that day," Amy said.

"Yes. He recognized it. Lucas is Ojibway. So was Him Standing. It must have seemed too good to be true for him," Sally said.

"Knight is a dark shaman?" I asked.

"Yes. But not one with true power. Not yet. He needs the mask."

"What about the mask?" Amy asked. "Why did Lucas carve his own face and not Him Standing's?"

"Him Standing lives in the dream world. Otter Tail did not tell him that the dream world and our world exist in the same time and place but do not meet. There is no doorway," Sally said.

"But that's what he said. *The doorway is open*," Amy said. "I heard Lucas say that."

"Lucas has changed, hasn't he?" Sally asked.

"Yes," Amy said. "It scares me."

"He goes to the dream world. There he is under the power of Him Standing. The dark shaman becomes real through Lucas. The more he dreams, the more he carves. More dark magic goes into the mask."

"I am the doorway," I said. "When it's finished, it will hold the spirit of Him Standing."

"And all of his power," Amy whispered.

"Yes," Sally said. "He is coming through you and into the mask."

"A spirit mask," I said quietly.

"There are good and bad spirits," Sally said. "Your grandfather did not teach you this. It is the weakness they looked for."

"This is really freaking me out," I said. "How are we supposed to fight something like this?"

Sally reached over and took my hand. "Finish the mask," she said.

"What if I can't?"

"What do you think might prevent you from finishing?"

"Fear," I said quietly.

"Fear is a magic of its own, Lucas."

"What do you mean?"

She smiled. "Fear is a power that we all have. Except we are never taught to accept it as a power. We get taught that it is a weakness. We are ashamed of it. We think it makes us less. But in fact it makes us more.

"It's only when we walk fully into it that fear shows its powerful side. The darkness isn't the absence of light. It's the threshold of light. When you are courageous enough to stand in your fear, you are learning how to step forward into the light."

I looked at the floor and considered what she'd said. "Are you telling me that if I finish the mask, even though it terrifies me to think about it, everything will be okay?"

"No," she said. "I'm telling you that you will be okay. That's what is certain."

"I still don't understand."

She took my hands in hers. "Walking through your fear makes you stronger. It makes you able to walk through other fears. It gives you courage. It gives you faith that there are bigger powers in the world than fear. When you walk through fear, you, Lucas, become a bigger power than the fear. It is its own medicine in the end."

"What do you mean?"

"The only way to conquer fear is by facing it."

I looked at her. She was calm. She was still and placid, and her hands were warm. She gave me a little smile, and I felt it in my chest. I trusted her. "I'll finish the mask," I said.

# TWELVE

I SPENT THAT NIGHT AT AMY'S FOR THE FIRST time. It felt good. We cooked supper. Then we sat on her balcony and watched the sun go down. After that we sat in candlelight and listened to music. Then we went to bed. We snuggled. We held each other. We fell asleep in each other's arms. For the first time since all of this started I didn't dream.

Amy had a photo shoot in the morning, so we got up early and went our separate ways. I took a long, leisurely ride through the city. The story Sally had told us made me jittery. But the ride through the city calmed me.

When I got to the rooming house, Gareth Knight was waiting in my room. I knew he would be there, but I faked surprise.

He was dressed like a punk. He had on black sneakers. He wore tight black jeans and a torn-up old black T-shirt. There was a black kerchief at his throat. He wore black eye makeup and black lipstick. His hair was spiked with gel. His arms were covered in tattoos made with black ink. They were of symbols I'd never seen before. He was sitting at my work table, drumming his fingers.

"Where have you been?" he asked, tilting his head and arching one eyebrow.

"Had to get out," I said. "Been working hard."

"Yes. But I need results, Lucas. Vacation on your own time. Now, where were you?"

"I told you I just needed to get away, that's all. I didn't go anywhere special."

"Ah. Ms. One Sky's, I take it. Where does the dear girl live, anyway?"

Sally had told me that he would want to know. "She has a place by the river," I said.

"It's a long river, Lucas."

"Well, she's becoming a famous model. She doesn't want just anyone knowing where she lives."

Knight smiled and rubbed at the tattoo on his forearm. "Don't get cute with me, Lucas."

Sally had told me that dark shamans existed on pride. They would never ask a question twice. It would mean they were weak. It would mean they didn't have power over someone. So I took a risk in order to protect Amy. "Hey, I'm not being cute. I'm just saying that you don't need to know where my girl lives. That's all."

"Ah, rebellion. I so love that energy. It feels so good to control." Knight stood up and stared at me. He raised a hand. I felt invisible fingers at my throat. Then I was lifted off the floor. I hung suspended three feet in the air. Choking.

Sally had told me too that anger was a dark shaman's weakness. If I could get him to express it, to reveal himself, he would have less of a hold. The grip he had was strong. I was scared. But knowledge is a weapon, and I held on to Sally's teaching. I waved a hand weakly in surrender. I was lowered to the floor.

I gasped and bent over to catch my breath. I could feel Knight waiting. I fought to get my breathing back. But I was happy to see him lose control. The other thing Sally had said was that it was important to get him to declare himself. If a wizard admitted who he was, he lost even more power.

"Neat trick," I said hoarsely. "Where'd you learn that, at some cheap magic school?"

"Cheap magic?" Knight asked. He sat back down on the chair and folded one leg over the other. "What I possess is not some party magician's bag of tricks. I'm not a buffoon, Lucas."

"What are you then?" I asked. "I know you're not just some moneyed-up art lover."

He smiled and scratched at his chin. He studied me intently. He nodded his head slowly.

"I'm a member of a very special club," he said. "Elite, really. There aren't a lot of us around."

"Big deal," I said. My voice was coming back. "I could say the same about me. There aren't a lot of guys like me around either. That's why you want me. I'm—what did you say? Elite?"

He laughed. "You're common. A dime a dozen. I could find someone like you on any street corner or any board-walk. In fact, I did."

"Yeah? So where do elite dudes like you hang out?"

"Hang out? We don't hang out, Lucas. We exist."

"So where do you exist then?"

Knight stood up. I could tell he was irritated. He shrugged his shoulders and shook his head and then spread his arms wide. He shook his hands. The room started to shake. My dishes rattled on the shelf. A few books tumbled. The air got hot, and it was hard to breathe. He rose slowly off the floor and spun lazily in a circle. Then he floated to the floor again. The room returned to normal.

He took a quick step toward me, and I shrank back against the wall. He smiled. He leaned in close to me. I could feel his hot breath on my face. His eyes locked with mine. They were dark and glittering.

"We exist on your fear, boy. We exist in your dark corners."

I grinned. I could see the rage in his eyes.

"Kinda vague for the elite. Don't you think?" I said.

Knight fumed.

"I am a shaman, if you must know. I am a grand wizard."

"So grand you gotta get a common person like me to

do your work for you? Carve your own mask then, Merlin."

I felt the invisible grip on my throat again. I was lifted off the floor again. He shook me, and I thought he was really going to lose it. I could see how far gone with anger he was. He fought to regain his calm, and I slid back to the floor.

"Finish the mask," he said firmly. "Or feel the force of my magic."

Then he turned and was gone.

# THIRTEEN

"SO YOU WERE ABLE TO GET HIM TO RISE TO anger?" Sally asked.

"More than that," I said. "The guy lost it."

"That's good. He needs the mask more than I thought. He needs it to give him a way to grab more power."

"He didn't seem to be short of any juice," I said, rubbing my throat.

"There is far more power to be gained than what he already has," Sally said.

"I can hardly wait," I said with a wince.

"What do we do now?" Amy asked.

We were sitting in Sally's backyard. She'd made a strong black tea that she said would give me the mental strength I needed to handle what was coming. That didn't sound so great to me, but I drank it anyway. It tasted awful. But something about the old lady told me I could trust her with everything. I did. Amy did too. We both drank our fair share of that rough tea.

"The good thing is that Knight has not been this way before. He has never found anyone with the gift your grandfather gave to you, Lucas. It means that even he does not know exactly what to expect. That's what our advantage is," Sally said. "We need to convince him that the spell and the hold of the dreams are working."

"They are," Amy said. "You told us that much yourself."

"Yes, but as long as Lucas comes to places of light, he is safe. The hold is broken for a short time, and that weakens it."

"So what are you saying?" I asked.

"I'm saying you need to be very careful. If Knight gets any idea that you have found a measure of safety, of light, you will be in great danger."

"Oh good," I said. "I thought you meant I had something to worry about."

Amy took my hand and squeezed it. Sally regarded both of us with concern.

"He may use the power he has now to imprison you, or worse. Dark shamans are soul stealers. You risk everything if you continue."

"Why don't I just disappear then? Take off. Split. Boogie."

"You can't," she said. "You know the truth. You know that the power of Him Standing can be brought into this world. If it is not through you, Knight will find someone else."

"Because I'm common. A dime a dozen, like he said."

Sally took both of my hands in hers and cradled them. She looked at the ground for a while. When she looked back up at me, she was crying.

"You are not common, Lucas. You are special. That's why Knight values you. You carry a gift. You are able to see the essence of things, their spirit. That kind of vision is not an everyday kind. But there are others. Knight will be drawn to their energy just as he was drawn to yours. Their fate will be the same."

"What fate is that?" Amy asked quietly.

There was a long beat of silence. We could hear traffic on the street, the birds in the trees, the wind. Sally raised her face and looked up at the sky.

"This world and the dream world are full," she said. "What is taken from one must be replaced by something of the other. There must always be a balance."

"Are you saying what I think you're saying?" I asked.

"Yes," she said quietly. "When the spirit of Him Standing enters this world, your spirit, or whoever Knight finds to do the work, will take his place. It will be imprisoned in the dream world forever."

"Oh my god," Amy said. "In limbo."

Sally could only shake her head.


THAT NIGHT I had a powerful dream. It started normal enough. But then it changed into something so sharp and real, I could still taste and feel everything about it when I woke up. I was walking across a wide prairie. The wind was blowing, and the sky was filled with clouds. They flew like giant sailing ships across the ocean of the sky. There were a few thousand buffalo grazing in the distance. I could smell them.

It was getting close to sunset. The western sky was on fire with so many colors, it was blinding. There was a fire in a small canyon. I could smell meat roasting. I could hear the wood crackling. I was suddenly very hungry, and I walked toward the fire. There was a man there wrapped in a blanket and poking at the fire with a stick.

As I got nearer, he turned to face me. I stopped dead in my tracks. Nothing moved in the dream then. There were no sounds and no smells. There was only the face of the man at the fire. My grandfather.

"Come sit, Grandson," he said. "I have been waiting for you. This buffalo roast is nearly ready."

I felt as though I floated to the fire. I couldn't feel my feet moving. When I got there, he waved me to a seat across from him and handed me a wooden cup filled with tea. It was Sally's tea. He smiled at me.

"How can you be here?" I asked.

"It is the dream world, Grandson. All things are possible here."

"My dreams have been scary."

"I know. But there are two sides, just as there are in your world."

"Light and dark," I said.

He nodded.

"In all things there must be balance. There are always two sides. Two faces." He looked at me solemnly as he spoke, and I realized for the first time in a long time how much I missed him.

He turned to the fire to tend to the meat. When he looked at me again, he was a young man. Then I watched as his face aged back to the one I remembered.

"Two faces, Grandson," he said. "To everything."

When I woke up, I knew exactly what I had to do.

# FOURTEEN

THE NEXT TIME KNIGHT SAW ME, I WAS IN horrible shape. I hadn't eaten. Hadn't washed. I was still wearing the same clothes he'd last seen me in. The bones jutted out from under my skin, which was yellow and sickly-looking. My eyes were red. They bulged like a madman's in a very haggard, worn face. I could hear the rattle of my breath in my chest. In spite of this, he smiled when he saw me.

"The work goes well, I see," he said. He was dressed in a black tuxedo with a black shirt. His shoes gleamed with a glossy sheen. His black cane rested on his thigh when he sat down to look at me.

"May I see it?"

"No!" I shouted and stood up quickly. I waved a fist in the air. "No one can lay eyes on this before it is finished. No one can see the doorway but me."

"My, my. You have been getting on, haven't you?" Knight said.

"I dream all the time," I said. "The vision gets clearer and clearer, and I can't stop working."

"Good. Good," he said. "You're under the spell of it."

"Yeah," I said and slumped back into my chair facing the work table. "He's so strong, so powerful. His face is incredible."

"He was a leader like no other. He was a magician. He could do things never seen before or since."

"A black shaman," I mumbled.

"That's what the fearful called him. What they call those of us who follow his teachings."

"He admires you," I said. I was staring at the cloth that covered the mask. I didn't blink. I stared and didn't move. I could feel him watching me.

"Does he now? And why would that be, Lucas?"

"No one has ever tried to call him forward before.

No one has ever thought it was possible. No one was ever a grand wizard like you."

"Well, I am truly honored to be held in such esteem," he said.

I turned to look at him. My face poured sweat, and I wiped at my eyes with a sleeve. I sat back in my chair with my legs spread wide. My hands dangled between my knees. My mouth hung open and my eyelids were half closed.

"He wants to live in you," I mumbled. A thin line of drool leaked from my lips.

"In me? I expected his power to reside in the mask."

There was a sudden chill in the room. It crept out from the walls, and we could see our breath. The lights flickered. They grew dim. The shadows in the corners seemed to move toward us. I could see Knight growing anxious. When I spoke again, the voice that came out of me was hollow. I didn't recognize it, even though I could feel my lips moving. "The boy was a poor choice. He is weak. He has no knowledge. There is no power in him."

"Master?" Knight asked. He leaned in to peer at my face.

"Whom else did you expect? The boy's hands have opened the doorway. It is as you wished to be."

"When, Master? When will you step through?"

"He inscribes a spell within the wood. The spell is the source of my power. It is the source of your own. The mask will contain it. Whoever wears the mask owns the power. When it is finished, I will come."

"Does he know? Does he have any clue to what we do?" Knight asked.

"Look at him. Does he look like one who has any wisdom?"

Knight studied me. He stared for a long moment, then waved a hand slowly in front of my eyes. I did not blink. I was locked in a trance. The only motion from my body was a twitching and another slide of drool from my mouth.

"He is not here," Knight said.

"He will not be. His dreams are my dreams. I send them to him. Even when he is awake, I send them. He lives in them now. This is how I give him the words to the spell he carves into the wood. He does not know anything."

"You're sure?"

There was a sudden roaring in the room. It was like the howl of an animal. But it was also like the screams of a horde of people in agony. It flew around the room in a circle. It echoed off every wall. It gained speed and volume. It became a tornado. Cupboard doors flew open. The closet door smashed against the wall, and the windows rattled in their frames. The lights went out, then flickered back to life. The room was a mess. The roaring died down.

Knight's face showed amazement. He looked at me where I dangled in the air, my arms hanging limply at my side. Then I spun in a slow, lazy circle, just as he had done. It seemed to take forever. Finally I was set down in my chair, and my head slumped forward onto my chest. Then my head snapped up again, and I stared hard at Knight. He cringed a little in his seat.

"You dare to question me?" The voice that came from me was savage.

Time seemed to stop.

"Who you are is because of me. What you know is what I have taught. Your power is my power. Do I need to convince you of this? Do you doubt who has power here?" The voice was huge and thundered in the room.

"No, Master," Knight said quietly. "I do not doubt you."

"Then leave me be. Let the boy finish what he has begun. I will summon you when the time is right."

"Yes, Master," Knight said and stood up.

He looked at me. I was slumped back in the chair. I heard him close the door, and then everything was silent. It was a long time before I could get back to the carving again.

# FIFTEEN

I'D NEVER LEARNED TO SPEAK OJIBWAY. BY THE time I was born, our lives had changed. The old ways were dying out. Most of the people around me when I was a kid spoke English. Anytime I heard someone say something in our language, it always sounded weird to me. Even on the playground and in the games we played as kids, we always yelled at each other in English. So I never got used to it. It was always something I kinda meant to learn when I had the time. I just never found that time.

So carving words into the inside of the mask was hard.

But it was hard for two other reasons, as well. The first was that they came while I was in dream time. The second was that there were a lot of them. It took a lot to carve them into the wood. And they weren't what I'd call words at all. They were symbols. They were these little scratchings and hen pecks that looked like things a kid would do.

I lost time. I disappeared. I bent to the wood with my chisel and knives, and the night would vanish. I don't know where I went. All I knew was that when I came out of it, I was tired. I could barely sit up in my chair. Now when I collapsed into my bed and slept, I slept without dreams. I just sank into it.

Most times it was noon or later when I came to. Once I got my feet under me, I made my way to Amy's. The place of light. The first time she saw me, she was shocked.

"My god, Lucas," she gasped. "What's happening to you?"

"I'm finishing the mask," I said.

"But your face. And your body. It looks as though it's eating you up."

"Feels like it too," I said. "What have you been doing?"

"Sally's been teaching me," she said.

"Teaching you what?"

"Stuff about our ceremonies. Things I never knew about how our people understood the universe."

"Secret stuff?" I asked.

She studied me for a long moment.

"No," she said finally. "Only stuff that we forget to ask about. I know that, living in the city, I forget about stuff like that."

"Me too," I said. "This whole thing's like a big giant puzzle to me, and I feel like somebody stole some of the most important pieces."

"Me too. It scares me, but it thrills me at the same time."

"How?" I asked.

"Well, it's kinda like you said—someone stole some of the important pieces. I feel like this is showing me what parts of my own puzzle I've been missing."

I looked out the window to think over what she had said. I felt better. I felt real. I felt safe, like the old lady had said I would. I let that feeling wash over me and fill me. When I looked at her again, I smiled.

"I never knew how incomplete I felt," I said and took her hand. "I dreamt of my grandfather. We sat together just like in the old days. I think he meant to give me those pieces, but he was gone before he had the chance. After that, nothing really seemed to matter anymore, and I left it all and came here. Now I know how much I walked away from."

"Does it make you sad?" she asked quietly.

"Yeah," I said. "Angry too."

"At yourself?"

"Not so much, but some at me for wasting it."

"You're not wasting it. You're carrying on your grandfather's gift. You're bringing it to a whole new group of people."

"I guess," I said. "But is that enough, you think? Does working without a foundation matter in the end?"

"It does if you bring your heart to it," Amy said. "You do that. It's what makes you great."

She smiled. I stood up and walked to her and gave her a hug. We held on to each other for a good long time without speaking.

"There's a secret I need to tell you," I whispered in her ear.

"Does Sally know?" she asked.

"Yes," I said. "She does."

# SIXTEEN

SALLY FOUND A SPOT FOR ME TO GIVE THE
mask to Knight. She said it needed to be a place that held
good energy. It had to be a place that was peaceful. Most
important, it had to be a place that he had never been
before. It had to be a place of light that didn't look like
one. When I told her I had finished the mask, she found
the spot in less than a day.

I left a note with directions for Knight in my room.
The three of us went to the spot to wait for him. It was
at a bend in the river about three miles beyond the city
limits.

"In the old days this was a gathering place," Sally said. She was wearing a pale buckskin dress with fringes, a plain red cloth head band and plain moccasins without beadwork. She looked like a grandmother. "The good hearts would gather here for ceremonies. When the city grew, it never seemed able to reach this place. It spread out in other directions but not in this one."

"No one knew its history?" Amy asked.

"Some could get it sometimes," Sally said. "But sacred places tell their story by feeling."

"Is that how you found this place?" I asked. "Or have you been here before?"

"It called to me," she said and smiled. "When I sent out good thoughts for a safe place for you to offer the mask, I felt this place. It was easy to find."

There were thick bushes around a clearing in the trees. The grass was about knee-high. The wind made a soft whisper as it moved through the leaves and the grass. The river gurgled at the far edge of the clearing. We could hear birdsong and the splashes of fish jumping. It felt like we were in a place that existed beyond time.

Sally directed me to press the grass flat with my feet in a circle in the middle of the clearing. I was carrying the mask in a big canvas sack, and she told me to set it on the ground in the middle of the circle I had made.

"When he comes, make him ask for it," she said. "He has to make a request for power."

When I'd finished, Sally and Amy picked out a spot in the bushes where they could not be seen. I was left alone in the clearing to wait for Knight.

It didn't take long.

He just appeared. One minute I was alone, the next he was there. There was the hint of a smile on his face. He wore black denim and cowboy boots. His hat was a neat little black bowler.

"I must admit, Lucas, I like the back-to-nature touch," he said. "It's fitting. Very noble-savage and all that."

"Well, after all this work, I need some fresh air," I said.

He pointed to the sack at my feet.

"That's it then?"

"Yes. I think you'll like the handiwork."

"Oh, it's more than mere handiwork, Lucas. It's magic."

"Magic takes a lot of work," I said.

"Yes," he said, stroking his chin. "Sometimes it does. May I see it?"

"Excuse me?" I said.

He tilted his head and grinned at me.

"How quaint. The artist struggles to let go of his creation. His baby."

"Something like that."

"Well, okay. Lucas, may I have the mask?"

"Sure," I said, smiling. "It was yours all the time. I made it for you."

I bent to retrieve the mask from the canvas sack. I caught a glimpse of Amy and Sally staring out at me from a break in the bushes. They were lying flat on the ground, watching. The fact that Knight did not know they were there gave me hope. He was not all-powerful. When I stood up, I held the mask behind my back.

"It didn't turn out the way I thought it would," I said.

"True art never does, does it?" Knight asked. He took a step closer to me, his hand outstretched.

"I suppose not," I replied. "But I never figured on carving this." I pulled the mask out from behind my back and held it out to him. It was a perfect copy of my own face, but I'd painted it black with three red wavy lines down the right side.

Knight's mouth dropped open. He took very slow steps toward me, and his hand shook a little as he neared the mask. I felt the wind stop. Everything went silent. The air grew thicker, heavier. I could hear the rustle of the grass with every step he took.

"The master," he whispered.

I put the mask in his hands. It was apparent that he had never seen the face of Him Standing and had no idea how the mask was supposed to look in the end. He stood with his head bent, and I thought I heard him sigh. He rubbed the symbols on the inside of the mask with the fingertips of one hand.

"The doorway," he said. "The words to open the doorway. When I put the mask to my face, they will be given to me."

"It's what the dreams told me," I said. "I put them there exactly as they came to me from the dream world."

"This is what my associates and I have wanted for a very long time," he said. "They will be pleased when I return with the master."

"With the mask, you mean?"

Knight raised his head and stared at me. There was a question in his eyes.

"I mean that when I put the mask to my face and open the doorway, the master will emerge," he said. "It is what is foretold."

"Maybe in your circles," I said. "In my circles, in my dreams, in my art, I was told to make this."

I went down on one knee and rustled about in the canvas sack. I looked up at Knight. He was watching intently. I slowly stood up, my back toward him. When I turned to face him, he was stunned by the second mask I wore on my face.

# SEVENTEEN

THERE WAS A SUDDEN ROLL OF THUNDER.
The sky was clear, but I heard the thunder clearly. Knight
glared at me. Behind him, the trees and bushes were swaying.
But there was no wind. I smelled something foul in the air.

"You dare to play games with me, Lucas? I have the mask
that opens the doorway," Knight said. He took a few steps
toward me, the mask held up to his face. "In a few moments,
none of this will matter at all."

I rubbed the face of the mask I was wearing. It was a
man's face. It was an old face. It was a face built of angles
and juts and shadows. It was a face with eyes that squinted

behind deep creases and lines. It was the face of a man who had known things—secrets, spells, charms, songs and prayers. It was the face of a shaman.

"You're not the only one with a mask of power, Knight," I said.

"Really?" he sneered. "Do you think you have what it takes to go against me? You know nothing."

"I know that you don't have enough juice to get Him Standing through the doorway on your own. If you did, you wouldn't have needed me."

"I told you. People like you are a dime a dozen. I would have found someone else who knows how to do a trick with a knife." He eased the mask to the side and smiled at me.

"Maybe," I said. "But no one who could have gotten the symbols you need. I did that."

"The symbols, yes. I confess that surprised me. But what surprised me more is the voice that came from you that day. It was clearly the master's voice."

Sally stepped out from behind the bushes. Her hands were behind her back, and she stood straight while the same energy that made the trees sway whipped her hair around.

"He's never heard the voice, Lucas," she said.

Knight spun around quickly. "Who is this? Another one of your little secrets, Lucas?"

Sally sidestepped carefully around him. Knight turned slowly, following her with his eyes. When Sally stood next to me, she took what she held behind her back and handed it to me. When Knight saw the large turtle-shell rattle, he screamed with anger. A sudden crash of lightning from the sky turned everything blue-white. When I took the rattle and turned to Knight, he was floating inches off the ground.

"I don't know who you are," he said to Sally. "But you are small and weak like him. Nothing you bring has the power to stop what I have put into motion."

Sally looked at him squarely. She didn't waver. She gazed at Knight, and I was proud of her courage.

"Raise the rattle," I heard her say.

I lifted the rattle up above my head. I felt my feet leave the ground. Knight and I now both hovered above the clearing in the trees. He laughed. Then he spun in a slow circle. It was my turn to laugh.

"I've seen that before, Gareth. It doesn't rattle me." I grinned at the bad pun.

"Maybe this will then," he said. He held both hands out toward me. Lightning bolts shrieked toward me.

I held the rattle out, and both bolts bounced off it and into the sky. Then I felt the taut strength of invisible hands at my throat. They squeezed. They were crushing. I began to feel the dark edge of unconsciousness. But there was something else. There was the face of the man I'd carved into the mask. He emerged from the darkness. His face hung suspended against nothingness.

"Move the rattle in a circle," he said calmly. "Shake it lightly in as wide a circle as you can."

My hands were weak, but I did as he said. As I made the circle in the air, I smelled the burn of lightning, and my feet touched down on the ground again. The grip on my throat was gone.

"Speak the words," the shaman said.

I began to say the words behind the symbols carved into the mask Knight wore. It was hard. I had never spoken the language. But I had heard them in the dreams while I carved the symbols, and I remembered the sound of them. I spoke slowly at first, unsure of myself, and Knight simply stared, his eyes wide with shock.

When I started to speak with more confidence, his expression turned to panic.

"What are you doing? How did you learn this spell?" he yelled. There was a sudden wind whipping around him.

"Dreams," I said, breaking off from the stream of words. I shook the rattle at him. "They are Otter Tail's words, and this is Otter Tail's face I wear."

"No!" he screamed.

He began tugging at the edge of his mask, but it wouldn't budge. He ran about in a circle, pulling at the mask with both hands. He collapsed onto the ground. He rolled about frantically. There was a cloud of dust around him as he wrestled with the painted mask latched to his face. He was screaming in fear.

I shook the rattle in a circle and kept on reciting the words. The wind spun into a tight circle. Knight was lifted off the ground.

Amy and Sally walked slowly toward me. We all watched Knight continue to struggle to get the mask off his face. They stood behind me as I continued speaking the ancient words. The wind grew wilder. Yet it blew only around him. Where we stood, it was calm and cool.

Finally he tired. He hung in the air, limp and wasted.

"How?" he croaked. "How is this possible?"

"You said it yourself, Gareth," I said. "I have the gift to open the doorway."

"But I wear the mask," he sputtered.

"You wear *a* mask. There are two faces to everything," I said. "All things must be in balance. This mask that I wear is the opposite of yours. When something comes out of the dream world, something must go back into it."

"No!"

"Yes. Your wish was to be one with your master. Well, now you can be." I shook the rattle in a wider, faster circle, and he spun in the air. I shook it faster and he spun faster. When his spinning matched the speed of the wind around him, he vanished like Him Standing had vanished long ago.

The wind died down. I collapsed. I could barely breathe.

I felt Sally removing the mask from my face. The air revived me. I opened my eyes, and Amy was kneeling at my side.

"Lucas," she said, "why didn't you tell me about Otter Tail when you told me your grandfather taught you how to fight this?"

"I couldn't risk Knight getting to you. I told you as much as I could and still keep you safe."

"You spoke the language."

"He gave it to me in the dreams."

"Him Standing never knew what you were doing?"

"It wasn't his dream," I said. "No one owns the dream world, Amy. No one owns dreams. They're for everybody. That's another thing my grandfather gave me."

"So Otter Tail was there all the time?"

"Yes."

"Waiting for you?"

"For someone," I said. "Knight said it best. I'm not the only one who knows how to do a trick with a knife."

# EIGHTEEN

AFTER KNIGHT WENT TO THE DREAM WORLD, my life settled down. I finally moved in with Amy, and I found an agent to help sell my work. I didn't need people as models anymore. I had dreams. But they were different now. They were filled with light. I was able to carve amazing things that shone like legends, and the wood seemed to take on a life of its own. My work was stunning and sold well. I had the money I used to dream about.

"You know, it's funny," I said to Amy one day.

"What's funny?" she asked.

"Well, all the stuff a guy dreams about—money, cars, big shiny things?"

"Yeah?"

"They feel better as dreams."

"What do you mean?"

I laughed.

"I guess I mean that now that I have some of that dream stuff, it doesn't matter as much as the other stuff I've found."

"What kind of other stuff?"

"All I have to do is look around me. I live in a great place all filled with light with a beautiful woman who loves me. I have a great career doing something I'm good at and that I love doing. I have friends. I have enough to eat. I can come and go as I please. And I still have dreams."

She smiled and took my hand.

"And these dreams you have now? What are they about?"

"Everything," I said. "Everything I ever imagined and everything I never imagined. It's what I carve now. What I imagine."

"The stuff of dreams," she said.

Now and then, my grandfather came to visit when I dreamed. We'd sit somewhere where the wind blew warm, and he would talk to me. He'd tell me all the things that he never got around to telling me when he was with me. He filled me up with legends and stories and teachings. When I awoke from those dreams, I felt very quiet inside. I felt humble. I never dreamed of darkness again.

I still took my tools and went to the boardwalk. I still hung out there a lot. But I found kids who wanted to learn how to carve, and I taught them for free. We sat in the sun with tourists standing around us, and I showed them how to bring wood to life. I gave them the gift my grandfather gave to me.

And sometimes, when those afternoons were over, I would go and stand at the end of the boardwalk and look out over the lake. I would stare at that point where water disappears into sky. I would marvel at how they flowed into each other. I would wonder how we sometimes miss seeing such a magical thing. Sometimes when I did that, I would see my grandfather's face or Otter Tail's in that space where everything came together. I knew that I could never ever be alone again.

Sally gave me the turtle-shell rattle. I gave her the mask. What she did with it we never knew, but she told us it was in a safe and honorable place. We trusted her. She became a good friend.

"You're a shaman, aren't you?" I asked her a month or so after Knight had gone to the dream world.

"Some people use that word," she said. "But it's not one we use to refer to ourselves."

"There are more of you?" Amy asked.

She smiled. "There are always people who seek to help others find their way."

"That's what a shaman does?" I asked. "What about the magic?"

"That is the magic," she said.

I believed her.

# THE NEXT SURE THING

# ONE

SO I'M WALKING OUT OF SHELLY'S CRAB Shack around 2:00 AM with a handful of bills from my tip jar, and the moon is like a freaking eyeball staring right down at me. I'm tired. Sometimes these gigs are more of a hardship than a blessing. But there never was a bluesman worth his salt that didn't have to pay his dues. Me, I figure a few nights working shabby rooms like the lounge in Shelly's is gonna be worth it once I hit. I have to hit. There's no way I can't. I got me a handful of sure-fire riffs born from the blues I carry in my bones, man. I was raised on a poor-as-hell Indian reservation smack-dab in the middle of nowhere, with twenty people sharing a three-bedroom house that had no glass on the windows and no electricity, and we had to haul the day's water from the lake in a five-gallon lard pail. So I know the territory of the blues. I been down so long it looks like up to me. That's how the old song goes, and I truly know how that feels. Trust me.

With a name like Cree Thunderboy, I'm a shoo-in. That's as honest a blues name as Lightnin' Hopkins, Muddy Waters or Sonny Boy Williamson. Getting folks to notice is the hard part. There's really no blues scene in this town. It's not really a working man's town. Ever since the high-tech boom, there's nothing but ISPs and systems-management joints or software-development places. And they mostly employ nerds and geeks who only listen to over-produced rock or pop or white-boy hip-hop. I busked for over a year on the sidewalk for nickels and dimes before Shel Lashofsky stopped to check me out on his lunch hour one day. He looked at me like I mattered. Like he cared what I was playing. So I vibed him out with some slick harmonica and some down-home thumping on the bass strings of my ratty old

Gibson, before peeling out a five-note run that would curdle cheese, man. That's how I got the gig at Shelly's, which is what Shel calls his place.

Trouble is, there's never anyone there. People come there to eat and head out to a shinier, more glamorous place. I wouldn't call Shel's a dump, but it's close. He serves up some good food, but he doesn't spend much on decor. Shel calls it realism. He says he's keeping it as close to Louisiana Cajun as he can even though, as far as I know, he's never been south of Ohio. So I plug in and play to six or seven people, maybe even a dozen on a good night. But a gig is a gig, and I don't sweat the lack of big tips. In fact, I'll take this handful of bills to the track tomorrow and turn it into a whole lot more. Fast.

When I first came here, I worked as an exercise groom for one of the big horse trainers. I'd have to be up at like four o'clock to get to the track before the sun was up, but I never minded. It was like going to school. I got a diploma in picking winning horses because I'd listen to the jockeys and the trainers talk about each day's race card and whose horses were right and whose weren't. I learned how to tell when a horse is ready just by looking at it. But you can't bet when you work the back lot, so I quit after six months. After that I just bet.

The only trouble with that was that the track got successful. Pretty soon there were new and bigger trainers with whole stables of horses I didn't know. There were a lot of new jockeys. So I was lost. I'd been winning for a while, but this new flood of activity left me high and dry. Even though I don't win a lot, I hit often enough to keep me going back.

My dad would say it's the lazy man's way. He was church-raised, a real Bible-thumper. And he didn't look kindly on either gambling or playing music. But the big bluesmen, the ones who left their mark, were all about playing the blues until the wee hours of the morning. When you do that like I do now, you get up late. It's hard to make an honest job when you don't get up until noon. Besides, to be a great blues player you have to be authentic, and this life I live gives me enough grit and hard times to make my music real.

Moms Mahood doesn't mind. Moms runs the rooming house where I live. It's not much. I got the only room with a small balcony overlooking the backyard, and I sit out there and play on evenings I'm not booked. All Moms cares about is if I have the rent come the end of the week. I've been late a few times, but I'm always good for it.

I'm twenty-three years old. I don't have a girlfriend. I don't own a car. But I can play a guitar that'll shuck the husk right off a cob of corn from fifty feet away. I'm going to be a bluesman. They're gonna say my name right along with John Lee Hooker and Howlin' Wolf and Stevie Ray Vaughan. That's my dream.

I'm going to win big money at the track too. That's my other dream. Because there's always a sure thing hiding in the numbers on the racing form. I don't know if that's true or not. I just choose to believe it.

# TWO

SO THERE'S THIS FILLY RUNNING IN THE THIRD race named Ocean's Folly. I keep staring from my race form to the tote board. I can't believe my luck. No one is putting any money on this horse, and her odds are sitting at thirty to one. That's a sixty-dollar payout on a two-dollar bet. When I check the numbers, I get excited. She's only run a few times, and from the looks of things, she's what a casual fan would call a "flier and die-er." In three of her four races she's run at the front, then fallen off coming around the last turn. But she has great early speed.

Now she's in a race with veteran horses, and not one of them is a nag. All of them have speed. The race is a mile long, and she's placed in the fifth position coming out of the gate. It gives her lots of room to move. According to the tote board, everyone seems to be choosing the favorite, a big roan gelding called Majestic Image. He's won three races over the last year at this same level of competition.

But what I see in the numbers is a young, fast horse trained for this distance. You could almost write off Ocean's Folly's first few races as training runs. She's just run to build up her familiarity with the distance. No other horse can match her for pure blazing speed out of the gate. As I scan each of her races, I see that she's been stretching that speed out. Now I see that the trainer and the jockey will let her have her head in the back stretch, and it'll be up to the field to try and catch her.

I'm so excited that my legs are bouncing up and down. The tote board numbers don't change on her. I have twelve dollars in tip money left after paying admission, buying a racing form and a program. Even if I only bet ten bucks, that's over three hundred dollars if she wins. I can't believe my luck.

"Got a hot one, do you?"

I look up, and there's a big, beefy white guy looking at me and smiling. He's got one leg crossed over the other and one arm across the back of the seat. The ring on his finger has to be worth a few grand. He's dressed to kill in a white linen suit and designer shoes.

"Nah," I say. "Not really. This one's pretty set with Majestic Image."

He nods. "Hard to go against his record. There's no cabbage in the action though. Odds are too low. Who do you like?"

"No one really."

"That's not what your legs say." He gives me a level look that I have to turn away from. His eyes are piercing. He stands and moves to sit beside me and offers his hand. "Win Hardy," he says.

"Win?" I ask.

"Short for Winslow. Never took much to that. Win feels better."

"Cree," I say, shaking his hand. "Cree Thunderboy."

He laughs. "Now that's a handle and a half. So who do you like, Mr. Thunderboy?"

"Maybe the nine horse. The odds are long, but in this

kinda race you have to go that way to make anything."

"You always bet to win?"

"Don't you?"

"Sometimes," he says and smiles. His teeth are dazzling. "Sometimes I just bet to learn."

"Expensive lessons."

"Maybe. But you can't put a dollar value on knowledge."

"What is it you hope to learn?" I'm not normally this open with strangers, but this guy just sort of oozes charm, and I can't help myself.

"People."

"Excuse me?"

He laughs. It's a low rumbling kind of laugh, manly and strong, and I like it.

"I like to learn people. I study them. I watch how they play, how they scrutinize, how they react to information. Like your leg. You were composed for a long time, and then the more you read, the more your leg got a life of its own. It's your tell."

"My tell?"

"Yeah. Like in poker. Everyone's got a tell, a subtle little sign when they sense a winner or get nervous."

"What's yours?"

He laughs again, sits straighter in his seat and looks out at the tote board. When he looks at me again, his face is blank as a stone. "I don't have one."

"I thought you said everyone did."

"Everyone but me, I meant. I never get nervous."

It was my turn to laugh, and when I did, he laughed too.

"Everyone gets nervous when it comes to money," I said. "Nervous to win and nervous to lose. It's your last bottom dollar that'll give you the blues."

"What is that, a poem?"

"Nah. It's a lyric. From one of my songs."

"Really? A songwriter? The blues, I'm guessing."

"You'd guess right then."

"Well, isn't that amazing."

"How so?"

He hands me a business card from an alligator-skin wallet. There's at least half an inch of money tucked in there. The card features a metal-flake comet in the top corner and says Win Hardy Talent Management. The card stock feels hefty, assured, confident.

"You're a talent agent?"

"Well, let's just say I have an interest in people that can make me money."

"At the track?"

"I've found that talent isn't limited to a specific area."

"What does that mean exactly?"

"It means if you tell me who you like in this race and convince me to like them too, I'll add to the ten bucks you've got to bet with."

"How do you know that ten bucks is all I have to bet with?"

He smiled again. "Well, for one thing, you just told me. For another, you're a blues player in a town with no blues scene, so you're not gigging much. Lastly, you have the look of someone looking for one good hit, not someone out at the track for an enjoyable afternoon in the sunshine."

"But you'd throw in with me if I tell you about this horse?"

He laughed and clapped me soundly on the back. It felt good. It felt all buddy-buddy and masculine. "See, I knew you had a line on something. So if it's not Majestic Image, who is it?"

I wound up telling him everything, and for some reason it didn't really surprise me.

# THREE

HE GAVE ME TWENTY DOLLARS, AND WHEN Ocean's Folly won by three-quarters of a length over Majestic Image, I collected almost nine hundred dollars. He did better than me. He won enough that they had to pay him by check. The first thing I did was pay him back the twenty. He studied me a moment, nodded, pocketed the money and led me upstairs to the clubhouse, where we sat on plush seats while a waiter served us drinks.

He sat back in his chair like a king. He spread both arms out over the backs of the adjacent seats and puffed on a long Cuban cigar. He had the expensive look of a Cadillac fresh off the lot. When he drank, he held the glass with a thumb and two fingers, and I thought it was a very delicate move for such a large man.

I watched people watch him. He had a way of drawing their eyes. It wasn't in any way I could determine. He just drew people. They couldn't stop looking at him. The men eyed him with envy, and the women offered coy looks over the tops of their programs or the rim of their drink glasses. I felt proud to be sitting with him.

"Well, Mr. Cree Thunderboy," he said. "That was very nice. Thrilling, even. You got any more aces up your sleeve?"

"Nothing that steps up and asks me to dance."

He laughed and waved at the waiter for fresh drinks. I never drank scotch. In fact, I hardly drank at all. It was the one bluesman thing I could never get a fondness for. I liked being clear. But the stuff he was buying was smooth and warm and smoky-tasting, and I liked it.

"Come on. You got the touch, kid. I can tell. Who do you like in the fifth?"

I shook my head. "No one."

"Come on."

"No. All the way up to the tenth, there's nothing. Sure things don't come around all that often. Most people think there's one in every box, as if life is like Cracker Jacks. It's not. You got to ride a lot of rail before the train hits the station again."

"You mix your metaphors. But I get you. You're saying, take the money and run. Grin all the way to the bank."

"I suppose. I never had a lot of loot in my time. So I tend to treat it carefully."

"Wise," he said. "I wonder, though, what you would do if you had a lot of loot, as you say?"

"That's not a bridge I'm likely to cross anytime soon."

"You tend to talk like a song lyric, do you know that?"

I laughed. "Comes with the territory, I guess."

"Yeah, well, if you stick with me, you might not be singing the blues too long. I can use a bright kid like you."

"I'm not a kid."

He turned and fixed me with that blank unreadable look again. The scotch left me able to hold it.

"You're right," he said. "You're not. I apologize. Figure of speech is all. I sometimes have too much of a Humphrey Bogart fixation."

"It's all right," I said. "But what do you mean, if I stick with you?"

"Well, Cree, I'm in the business of making money. I hire people who can do that for me. People with a talent. People with a dream. They work for me and use their talent, and I make their dreams come true."

"You've never even heard me play."

"No, but you know how to pick a winner. That's the talent I want. You do that for me, and I'll get you into a recording studio and promote your music. Hell, I'll even ante up for a video. The whole works. You just need to make your other talent available to me."

"For how long?"

He reached out an arm and clenched me around the shoulders. I could feel the bulk of his muscles and the strength of him. "Time is relative where loot is concerned."

"You can actually do all that? Recording, videos?"

"I have certain friends who can make certain things happen."

"There's no way I can find you a winner every day."

"Maybe not. But you do it often enough, like you just did today, and I'd be a happy man, and my friends would be too. Everyone likes the easy money. Keeps things simple."

It made me uncomfortable. Still, the idea of actually getting into a recording studio and making the album I'd always dreamed of was too hard to resist. His confidence was magnetic. "So what do I do?" I asked.

"You get the form, you make your pick, you come down here, check out the animal, and if it looks good, you go."

"With what? I'm a ten-dollar bettor."

He reached into his wallet and handed me a quarter inch of hundred-dollar bills. "Let's just call this an advance on your commissions. Your grub stake. You work the sheet tonight. Call me. I get the money to you. You come here, make the bet and bring me the winnings. Easy."

"How do I reach you?"

"The number's on the card. And here's a phone." He reached into his jacket pocket and handed me a small cell phone. "The number's speed-listed. Just press *One*."

"You carry phones to give away to people?"

"They're phones for my talent. I'm telling you, Cree, I take care of details. You take care of your end, I'll have your album out in no time."

"Sounds too easy."

He laughed. "The best things always are. And what you said about sure things? Sometimes they just walk right up and introduce themselves."

# FOUR

ASHTON CROOKER IS MY BEST FRIEND. He used to bring his djembe drum and give me rhythm backup while I played on the street. The funny thing about that is we never talked the first three times. He'd just show up, drum behind me and leave. He never asked for any of the tips. It always seemed like he found joy in the playing and that was all he wanted.

So one rainy day when there wasn't a lot of action, we headed for a coffee joint to warm up. We found out that we shared a passion for music. Ashton liked all kinds and filled my ears with talk of African, Brazilian and Cuban bands and drummers I should hear. We'd sit around his bachelor apartment and listen to music and talk long into the night sometimes. I told him about my life on the reservation and how the blues just reached out and touched me. He told me about growing up poor in a trailer park on the outskirts of Montreal and how drumming always seemed to make him feel better. He said he could even drum away hunger. That was the power of music. We were friends after that.

Now we sat in the same coffee joint, and he looked at me wide-eyed. "So he just gave you all this money?"

"Yeah. Just over three thousand."

"Commission?"

"That's what he said. An advance."

"That's too radical to be real." Ashton studied the card Hardy had given me. "Did you even call this number? See if it's a real office?"

"No. Why would I? The guy just wants fast money. Who doesn't? I mean, if I met a guy like me and figured he could get me some easy winnings, I'd go for it too."

"You'd hand off three grand to a stranger?"

"Well, maybe not that. But it shows he's got money.

Guys with that kind of money have connections, and he said he'd get me a recording session."

"I'd be careful about who his connections were."

"You know what, Ash? I don't even care. If it gets me into a studio, that's all I want."

"Yeah, but nobody's real name is Win."

I riffled the edges of the bills. "I won this."

"Maybe so," Ashton said with a worried look. "But guys like you and me, Cree, we don't get breaks like this. Not this easy. We're working-class guys who play a little music. Dream, yeah. But stay real, buddy. Stay real."

Just then the door opened, and two very large men walked in. They had heads the size of basketballs and eyes that stared straight ahead, unreadable like the eyes of dolls. They strode right over to our table and stood there looking down at us. I was suddenly very scared.

"Which one of you is Thunderboy?" the biggest one asked.

His friend punched him in the shoulder. "Well, gee, Vic. Would it be the Indian guy or the pasty-faced white guy? Hmmm. I wonder."

"Yeah, yeah, yeah," the one named Vic said. "Mr. Hardy

asks that you sign these papers." He held out a sheaf of legal-sized papers to me.

"What are they?" I said. "And how did you know where to find me?"

"Personal services agreement. Standard talent stuff," the other one said. "And we can always find you. Trust me."

Ashton and I exchanged a look. "Can I read them over?"

"I told you, standard stuff. You agreed in principle when you took the advance. So just sign the papers. We got work to do."

"What kind of work?" Ashton asked.

"Tell him, Vic."

Vic straightened up and stood as tall as he could and cast a sweeping look around the café. Then he leaned forward, his full weight on his arms. We could feel the tabletop bend. He looked right at Ashton with those bright, depthless eyes.

"Me and Jerry are commission agents. Thunderboy here pays us, we pay him. We get to be friends, have a few drinks. Maybe take in a ball game now and then. He don't pay us, the story takes a slightly different tack. You get my drift?"

"I get it," Ashton said. "I get it." He slid back in his chair.

I signed the papers and handed them to Jerry, who folded them without looking. He put his hands in his pants pockets, and his coat flapped back to reveal the butt of a gun in his belt. We stared at it. Hard. When we looked up at him, he was grinning.

"Sometimes things get tough in the commission business. We wouldn't want that to happen to you, Wonderboy."

"That's Thunderboy," I said.

"Same difference from what I hear. Be ready at nine AM. We'll pick you up."

"For what?"

Jerry slapped Vic playfully on the back, and the bigger man curled up his fists and ducked his head and shoulders down in a boxer's shuffle step.

"For what, the kid asks."

"Dumb kid," Vic said and stood beside Jerry. "You signed the deal. You should know the play. We pick you up in the morning and deliver you to the studio, where you cut some tracks. I hear you're some kind of whiz kid on guitar."

"I'm recording? Just like that?"

"Just like that, like it says in the deal," Vic said. "Then in the afternoon we deliver you to the track and you do your thing for the boss man. Here's tomorrow's form."

He laid the racing form on the table. Ashton and I both stared at it without moving. This all seemed to be happening very fast. The two large men watched us. When we didn't offer a response, they turned and walked toward the door. Then Vic turned on one heel and marched back, irritated.

"Don't forget to do your homework. The man needs your call before we pick you up. Got it?" he asked.

"I got it." I said. "I got it."

Ashton and I looked at each other a long time without speaking.

# FIVE

MOMS MET ME AT THE DOOR WHEN I GOT home. She was the next thing to giddy. I'd never seen her so happy. When I walked through the door, she hugged me, and I could feel her shaking.

"Are you okay?" I asked.

"More than okay," she said and stepped back to look at me. "It's so amazing what something like a little prayer can do."

"What do you mean?"

"I mean my sister has been off work for a year after her hip operation. Things weren't looking very good, and she really needed money just to get by while she was off her feet. This place keeps me going, but it doesn't give me extra to pass around. But I prayed and asked for a way to help. And the next thing you know, your boss, Mr. Hardy, shows up and pays a whole year in advance."

"He did that?" Things were happening too fast.

"Yes. He just left a half hour ago."

The cell phone in my pocket rang, and I walked out onto the porch to take the call.

"I take it you're home by now." There was a touch of a laugh in Hardy's voice.

"How did you know where I live?"

"I'm the kind of guy who likes to know everything about the people he hires."

"That's not an answer."

"It is in my book."

"Not in mine," I said.

"Well, the thing is, Cree, you're not writing the book. I am. You're walking around with a fistful of my green. And you got a date to lay down some tracks in a studio just like you always wanted to do. What's with the attitude?"

"I don't like being followed."

"No one's following you. I just like to know where my money's walking to when it walks out the door."

"Are you happy now?"

"Extremely. Nice lady, that landlady of yours. Seemed happy to have a little extra to work with. Glad I could help."

"I didn't ask you to pay my rent."

"No need. I'm your new BFF."

"Best friend forever?" I asked, irritated.

"Best friend with firearms. Just remember that." The phone went dead in my hand.

I sat in my room mulling over the events. Suddenly I didn't like Hardy much. Beyond the charm and the dazzle was a coldness that worried me. His henchmen were buffoons, but there was a hard ugliness behind their playful natures. Still, the roll of bills felt good in my hand.

My guitar and small amplifier stood in the corner, and the idea of finally making it into a recording studio excited me. But there was pressure I didn't need. The odds of finding a sure thing were long enough without the added weight of having to keep Hardy happy and avoid the dark side of his goons. I didn't like owing him. I didn't like feeling kept like a dog on a leash. I didn't like the threat hanging over me.

But the blues is built of stories of men who make deals with the devil. And the glitter of promise I saw outweighed the bad feelings in the end. I unfolded the racing form and lay back on my bed to study it. At least I got to play with my strong suit.

There wasn't a lot of action the next day. As hard as I studied, nothing emerged that smelled anything like a winner. At least, not in the big way of Ocean's Folly. People never seem to realize that winning big takes a lot more than just knowing what to look for in the racing line. You need to know the variables. What a horse looks like by the numbers has little to do with how they look in the post parade. There's taping and liniment, the way they move, the set of their ears, if they're wearing blinders. Even the condition of the track and the weather make a difference. The numbers only get you so far, and the way they read, there was nothing to really move on.

After three hours, there was only one thing to do. There was a horse in the seventh named Sports Day, and he was listed as a five-to-one shot. That would pay a mere ten dollars on a two-dollar bet. But if a guy were to lay down a thousand, it would mean a payout of five thousand.

The trouble was that Sports Day was going up in class. It meant that he would be racing stronger, more experienced horses. But his workout times impressed me, and the race was a sprint. Six furlongs. He'd raced at a mile at the lower levels and always been very quick in the first half mile. It was worth a shot, if a guy had an extra thousand to lay down. I did, but the idea made me nervous.

This was no sure thing. It was a risk. Hardy wanted bets that would cash out, and there was no way of knowing whether this one would make the cut. I decided that I would use some of the advance money and make the bet myself. I'd tell Hardy there was nothing going on the race card that day. I could learn something betting big money and not have to risk losing Hardy's cash and maybe not being able to record my songs. That was the most important thing. When you get this close to a dream, you can't let it go. You can't.

I told myself that move was all about education. I told myself it was preparing me for doing what Hardy wanted me to do. I told myself it was okay. Still, I didn't sleep much that night. Playing big money will do that to you.

# SIX

THE RECORDING ENGINEER WAS A GUY named Keys. They called him that because he'd been a hot keyboard player when he was young and had actually toured with some big-name jazz groups. But he developed arthritis in his hands. Keys knew his way around a soundboard though. And he knew how to talk to musicians and how they liked to work. I felt comfortable right away. He set me up behind some wooden sound baffles with a stool and a microphone and my guitar plugged into an old Fender tube amp. He said it would give my riffs a good old-time sound. It did.

We laid down five songs that morning. I'd only ever heard myself on cheap tape recorders before. The way the studio recording sounded made me feel ten feet tall. The guitar runs were crystal clear, and when I vamped the chords, they were all fat and thumpy like the old-time bluesmen. My voice sounded raspy and growly and very blue.

"We got something here," Keys said. "It's bluesy, jazzy, very funky. I like it. You write good stuff."

I'd never felt prouder.

Vic and Jerry hung around for the whole session. They hadn't been too happy when I told them there was nothing to bet that day. They were less impressed when I booked out of there alone.

"The boss won't like this much," Vic said. "Things are a little one-ended here."

"Well, what would you have me do? Lie to him? Lay down dumb money just so he's happy knowing there's action?"

"Maybe not. But you have to give him the word. Not me."

Vic punched in some numbers and then handed me the phone. Hardy answered right away.

"Yeah," was all he said.

"It's me. Cree."

"Hey, Wonderboy. How's the action looking?"

"Well, if it was my money, I'd keep it in my pocket today."

"Why?"

"There's nothing. Everything's a toss-up. I wouldn't put your cash out there."

"You're not just saying that?"

"No."

There was a silence at the end of the line. Vic and Jerry eyed me. I shifted from foot to foot, waiting.

"Okay," he said finally. "You're the man. I trust you. Take the day. Spend some loot. Have a little fun. I'll talk to you later."

I handed Vic the phone, and he mumbled into it. Then broke the connection and shrugged.

"Guess you can go," he said.

"With your permission," I said.

"Don't get cute, kid. Ever."

I took that as my cue to leave.


ASHTON WASN'T EXACTLY impressed with my thinking. He sat there while I told him my plan and shook his head slowly. Then he looked up at me and stared for long enough to make me nervous.

"This guy sounds like trouble if things don't follow his line," he said finally.

"I know that. But the thing is, Ash, I gotta show him that I know how to think too. Right now he's making all the moves and taking control. I don't want him thinking I'm just a flunky."

"Okay, but are you prepared to handle it if he flips out because you acted on your own?"

"He asks me to act on my own."

"To pick the horses, yeah. Not to venture out without telling him."

"I don't see the problem."

"You won't until after." He picked up his coffee and took a long slow sip. "But I'm still gonna go with you."

"Why?"

He laughed. "I've never seen anyone lay down a thousand bucks on a bet before. Nor have I watched anyone have to watch their money run around a track."

"Glad I entertain you."

By the time we got to the track, the grandstand was

full. We'd missed the first four races, and the action for the fifth was fast and heavy, according to the numbers on the tote board. We picked up some burgers, Cokes and a racing form and found a quiet area that overlooked the paddock area so we could see the horses when they arrived prior to their race. Ashton liked to people-watch. He sat and ate and looked over the crowd while I thumbed through the form. I was so nervous that I had trouble reading. Finally I put the form down and ate my burger while I watched the horses and jockeys get ready in the paddock. Just for something to do, I walked to the window and put a ten-dollar bet on a big roan gelding called Falmouth's Boy. I never made pointless bets, but I was antsy. I needed a distraction. Ashton followed my lead and bet five dollars on the same horse. He won by half a head.

"How'd you know?" Ashton asked as we cashed out.

"I guessed," I said.

"Good guess."

"Yeah. But I never do that. It's being foolish."

"Foolishness just made me fifteen bucks."

"Yeah, well, luck is luck, I guess."

"Hope your luck holds out in the seventh."

We killed time until the horses paraded for the seventh and I got a chance to look at Sports Day. He was muscular and fit-looking but smaller than the rest of the field. There was a knot of anxiety in my gut. I fingered the roll of bills in my pocket and toyed with the idea of just forgetting it and waiting until I could find a sure thing for Hardy. But I needed to show him that I was independent, that I could operate on my own. I didn't like feeling owned. This was my chance to gain a little freedom. With three minutes to post time, I walked up and made the bet. My hands shook while I counted out the bills. My mouth was dry, and I gulped down a Coke. There was no way I could sit to watch the race, so we stood at the rail at the edge of the second-floor seats. Ashton watched me worriedly.

"You gonna be okay?"

"I hope so."

When the horses charged out of the starting gate, Sports Day was almost invisible behind the larger horses. But his size let him slip between them, and he found daylight. The gate was at the foot of the backstretch, and I could see him race into the far turn, leading by half a length. I thought I would faint. He led through the turn, and then a pair of bigger horses made a move and drew even with his shoulder. Down the homestretch, there wasn't an inch to separate them. Every lunging stride seemed to push one of the three ahead. The crowd was wild. I leaned on the railing and clutched it hard. Time slowed. Everything seemed to move in slow motion. I could hear Ashton yelling in my ear, but the words didn't register. My hands hurt from gripping the rail.

When the horses flashed across the finish line, Sports Day had won by a nose. I wobbled to a seat and flopped down in it. I could barely breathe. I put my head on my forearms and swallowed huge gulps of air. When I looked up, Ashton was smiling at me.

"You just won five thousand dollars," he said.

I still hadn't got my breath back when we returned to the counter for the winnings.

# SEVEN

YOU WALK A LITTLE DIFFERENT WHEN YOU carry a check for five grand in your wallet. There's a casual flow to your stride and you feel like walking is easier. You feel light-headed and you breathe shallower. And if you close your eyes, you get the feeling that you might just float away. That's how I felt as Ashton and I walked away from the racetrack. I'd never won so much before. But then, I had never bet so much either. My nerves were frayed and I was still jittery. But I was full of energy—vibrating, really. I wouldn't have changed those feelings for anything.

"That was freakin' awesome," Ashton said. "Thrilling, scary, wonderful all at the same time."

"I thought I was going to lose it at the end," I said.

"Jeez. He only won because he exhaled when the other horses inhaled. That's how close it was."

"Tell me about it." I was still lost in the thrill of the race and that heady feeling that comes when you're so excited you forget to breathe.

The day was suddenly sunnier and warmer than it had been before. I laughed and punched Ashton on the shoulder. He winced and grabbed at it, but he laughed too. We walked faster toward the bus stop. We were shaking our heads and talking about what we'd do with the rest of the day when a black Lincoln Navigator swung in across the sidewalk in front of us. Neither of us was too surprised when Vic and Jerry stepped out.

"Both of you. In the back," Jerry said. His hand was in the front of his blazer.

Ashton was pale. I looked at Vic, and he just shook his head at me and held out one hand to the open back door of the SUV. We climbed in. The silence was hard. Neither of them spoke at all. Vic drove, and Jerry sat staring straight ahead. Ashton and I fidgeted nervously while we made our way through downtown traffic. Finally we pulled up behind a long red-brick warehouse.

"Get out," was all Jerry said.

They walked us in the back door. It looked like an auto parts place. There were long rows of shelving where workers were gathering items and boxing them to place on conveyors that carried them to other workers, who loaded them onto trucks at a pair of loading docks. No one bothered to look at us as we passed. We were marched up a set of stairs and through a set of offices with secretaries busy with paperwork. The silence was the worst. Neither Vic nor Jerry spoke all that time. They just walked solemnly behind us. We could feel the weight of their big bodies following us, and we walked as fast as we could. We ended up in a paneled office with floor-to-ceiling windows overlooking the street. Vic motioned us to sit on a leather couch along one wall. They went to stand at either side of the door.

Hardy entered through a side door. He walked to his desk without looking at us or speaking. When he sat, he drank from a tumbler and eyed me over the rim. Then he put it on the table softly—so gently it gave me the creeps.

He folded his hands in front of him and leaned forward in his chair.

"Never did much care for freelancers, Cree. I expected some degree of loyalty from you." He leaned back in his chair.

"I don't know what you mean," I said.

"You took my money and made your own play. You left me out of the loop. I call that a total lack of respect."

"That's not what happened."

He stood up suddenly. He leveled a hard look at me.

"You take a grand of my money and put it to work and you don't tell me about it? You pick up five grand, and you're gonna walk off and play like nothing happened? Like you didn't use my generosity for your own end? Don't play me, Cree. We know what you did."

"You had me followed?"

"You think I don't have people at the track? I knew as soon as you got there, and I knew when you made your play. Nice trick though. Waiting until just before the bell went off to lay down your wager. Makes it hard for anyone else to get in."

"I waited because it took me that long to be sure."

"Sure of what? That you were in the clear?"

"No," I said and stood up too. Vic and Jerry took a half-step forward. "To be sure that it was the right move."

"It wasn't," Hardy said. "You used my money. You cheated me."

"Our deal was for me to let you know when there was a sure thing," I said. "This wasn't. This could have gone totally the other way." I looked at the goons. They spread their legs wider and clasped their hands in front of themselves and rocked on the balls of their feet. "I didn't tell you because I didn't want you to risk your money. So I used the cash you gave me because you said it was mine. That way if I lost, it was my loss. I didn't think you thought it was still yours."

"You still made a play without telling me. Disobedience doesn't earn you any points, Cree. It just earns you pain. Or it earns your friend pain." He nodded to Vic, and the big guy reached over and hauled Ashton to his feet by the scruff of his neck. There was a large knife in his hand. Ashton looked ready to faint. Vic held the knife to his ribs and looked at Hardy.

"Ever wonder why they use the term 'blood money,' Cree?" Hardy asked.

"No," I said nervously.

"Because it's earned by blood. Your pal's blood, unfortunately. You want to mess with me? This is how you pay for that."

"Why?" I said and took a step forward. I heard Jerry move with me. "Because I took a risk without involving you? Because that risk paid out? Because I took a counter check from the track with your name on it?"

Hardy looked stunned. "What did you say?"

"You heard me. The check's made out to you."

"You kidding me?"

"Look for yourself." I held the paper out, and Hardy stepped around the desk and took it.

"Well, damned if it isn't," he said.

"I know about loyalty," I said. "You got me into a studio where I laid down five tracks for an album. You gave me the first installment on my dream, and I took this risk because it wasn't a sure thing. I thought you gave me that money without strings. I didn't want to risk your cash. This way if I lost, it was my loss, not yours. That's what I figured."

Hardy smiled. "I knew you were a good kid."

He reached out and shook my hand. He held on to it tightly and looked over my shoulder and nodded at Vic, and I could hear Ashton collapse onto the couch.

"But don't ever make a move without telling me again," he said. "Not even a small one. If you know about loyalty, you'll take care of your friend."

All I could do was nod.

# EIGHT

WE SAT AT A SMALL SIDEWALK CAFÉ. ASHTON, Hardy and me. Vic and Jerry sat in the Navigator a few yards down the street. It was warm in the late afternoon. The café was filled with people chatting and laughing. There were plates of appetizers in front of us and glasses of good white wine. But neither Ashton nor I were much in the mood for food or drink. Hardy ate triumphantly. He eyed me over his fork, then set it down and wiped at the corner of his mouth with a napkin.

"I got friends that want to meet you," he said.

"I have friends," I said.

"Not like these. These are friends that can make your world. Or break it just as easily."

"Why would I want to meet people like that?"

He smiled and drank some wine. "Mostly because you don't have a choice. See, I work for these guys, and they're interested in your talent too. While you were waiting for me in the car, I told them about your five-to-one shot and how you played it. They like your moxie."

"Moxie?"

"Yeah. Balls. You know."

"I don't."

"Everyone gets scared, Cree. The trouble is that most people don't move through it. It cripples them. Not you. You push through it. Even if you piss people off. That's moxie, and my friends want it working for them."

"I don't work for anybody."

Hardy spun his wineglass slowly in his fingers. "You work for me."

"I thought we had a deal."

"The deal is you work for me. And you work for my friends. That should be clear by now."

"I think I want out."

Hardy laughed then. It was genuine. As though no one had ever told him quite as big a joke before. He fumbled in his coat for his cell phone and punched in a number on speed dial.

"Kid says he wants out," he said into it and smiled at me and shook his head. "That's what I did too. Cracked me right up. Hey, he's a green kid, never done nothing in his life. What do you expect?" He listened for a moment and a deep line appeared in between his eyebrows. He nodded, then looked at Ashton and handed him the phone.

"Guess you get to translate, buddy boy. My friend would like to speak to you."

"Me? Why?"

Hardy chuckled. "Ask him."

Ashton gave me a quizzical look and held the phone up to his ear.

"Yes?" he said.

I watched his face change. It went from curious to worried to shocked right in front of me. He held the phone so tightly that his knuckles went white, and he breathed through his mouth like a kid. I could hear a thin seam of voice from the phone. It was regular, straight, without rises or changes in pitch or volume. Ashton just listened, and when he handed the phone back to Hardy, he couldn't look at me.

"Tell him," was all Hardy said. He said it coldly. Ashton stared at him a moment before turning to me.

When Ashton looked at me, his face looked like he'd been slapped. It was white and strained.

"Leo Scalia," he said.

"Excuse me?" I said.

"Leo Scalia," Ashton said again, more urgently. "Hardy works for Leo Scalia. He runs book for the mob. Hardy's connected. He's made. You can't quit."

I looked at Hardy, who sat back in his chair with his legs crossed, grinning at me. "You're connected?"

"Big-time," he said. "But hey, my friends are your friends, Cree. You're our pony now. Or at least, you're mine. Quitting? Well, no one likes a quitter, do they?"

"I can't do this," I said.

"Can't do what? We're only asking you to do what you already know how to do. This is no stretch. Hell, if you want, you don't even have to carry any action. You don't have to make the bets. You just make the tote, give us the number. We play the horse, and you get your commission and our endless high regard. Besides, I own the paper on your whole friggin' life. So what's 'can't do'?"

"What are you talking about?" Ashton was shaking his head beside me. Hardy waved a hand in the air. I heard the doors of the Navigator slam and the footfalls of Vic and Jerry. Hardy stood and shrugged and straightened his jacket with both hands. Then he leaned forward on the table toward me. His eyes were hard. I could smell cigar smoke and wine. He put one knuckle under my chin and lifted my head. I heard the goons step up behind me.

"Call me your proud new papa, Cree. I paid your rent. I'm footing the bill for your first album and video. You want new gear? You got that too, because I got you a gig at the Purple Onion starting next week. You'll need a bigger amp, and me, I figure the blues sounds best on a Gretsch semi-hollow body with a nice stack of Fender amps behind it. Red, maybe. I like red. What you think, Jerry?"

"Red is good, Win. Real good," Jerry said from behind me.

"And if you do ever decide to get cute, Cree? Call your folks on the rez. Ask 'em how they like the new truck.

Ask your sister how she likes having her tuition paid for. I own all of them. Not just you. So your moves are their moves now. Remember that next time you think you can quit on me. Vic? Give him tomorrow's form."

He let my chin go, grinned at me and gave me a light playful slap on the cheek.

"He's a good kid. Green, but good," he said to Vic and Jerry. Then he turned and walked away.

Ashton and I sat there in silence. I was stunned. "Can it get any worse?" I asked.

"Yeah," Ashton said. "It can."

"How's that?"

"I didn't tell you what else he does for Scalia."

I looked at him. He looked sad and scared. "Are you kidding me?"

"No," he said. "He's a collector. A knee-breaker."

I suddenly felt like drinking the wine. All of it.

# NINE

AS IT TURNED OUT, HARDY'S PEOPLE HAD been to the reservation. They'd arrived in a row of three black SUVs and made a big display of friendship. My family was told that Hardy was my boss and that I was working as an investment counselor. I was doing such a bang-up job that he wanted to reward me as much as he could, and helping to take care of my family was the way he had chosen. Somehow he talked the chief and his councilors into giving my family a house of their own. He furnished it too, as well as parking a new half-ton pickup truck in the driveway. All of this was fine with my father. When I'd walked away to pursue the vague dream of being a blues musician, he hadn't been thrilled. But with the arrival of Hardy's people and the outlay of goodwill cash, he seemed more willing to believe that I was actually worth something in the world.

"You work hard for this man," he said over the telephone. "He can obviously do a lot for you."

I couldn't tell him what the real score was. He had the new house, the truck and furniture, and my sister had her tuition paid for at the college where she was studying nursing.

"They left a thousand dollars that they said you would earn back in no time too," my father said. "That kind of man is someone you hold on to. Anyone can see that."

Ashton just looked at me blankly when I told him later at the coffee joint. He hadn't said much since the encounter with Hardy and the knife at his ribs. I was worried about our friendship.

"There's got to be a way to get out from under all this," he said. "I just don't know what it is."

"I'm sorry, Ash," I said.

He shook his head.

"It wasn't your fault. These guys look for people to trap all the time. They don't have the skill set or the brains to do anything themselves. How were you to know the guy was bad?"

"I should have been more careful."

"You were doing what you do. There was never any inkling that it would go sour."

"Well, it has. Now he has my family in his pocket. They all figure he's the best thing that ever happened to me. But what scares me is how much he knows about my life and how much of it he controls now."

"He's got your back to the wall. What bothers me is the threat."

"Yeah. Everything I do, win or lose, means someone close to me will get hurt."

"Or killed," Ashton said. "They're talking big money here now. Leo Scalia doesn't play around."

"So what do I do?"

"Make your record. Make your bets. Hope for the best."

"Hope for the best?"

"I guess. There's no way out that I can see."

"How big is Scalia?"

"He's the biggest player in this town. I don't think he's got much reach beyond that, but he has his fingers in a lot of pies. There are a lot of people who only move when he lets them move."

"Like me?"

"Like you."

"For now."

He looked at me, and I could feel him searching me for a clue to what I was thinking. The truth is, I didn't really know for sure what I was thinking. I only knew that this wasn't the way the dream was supposed to go. As thrilled as I was about being able to record my album and the plans for shooting a video to put up on YouTube and maybe attract some attention from the big boys in the music biz, I hated the idea of being owned like a prize cow or something. It irked me that I couldn't make a move without Hardy now. The fact that he worked for a criminal, and that he wasn't shy about causing pain or even getting rid of people who wronged him or stood in his way, made me feel that Hardy, with his oozing charm, was evil. The devil. Or at the least, a major demon. I wanted to exorcise him from my life somehow.

"He's gotta have a weakness," I said.

"Sure," Ashton said unconvincingly. "And a couple of shlumps like us are going to find it and bring him down?" He took a long drink of his coffee and drummed his fingers on the table, watching me.

"Sounds impossible, I know. But someone like Hardy has to have hurt somebody along the line. He can't go through life pushing people around without there being someone somewhere who wants to get back at him."

"True enough, I suppose," Ashton said. "But how are we ever going to find that person? I'm no detective. Neither are you."

I stared out the window at the street. There were a lot of people out enjoying the sun and the warmth, and everyone looked happy and busy. They seemed so casual. They walked as though they had no worries, no cares, no burdens. It felt like a blues song to me and made me feel even more trapped. I scribbled a line of lyric on my napkin.

"What are you doing?" Ashton asked.

"Just scratching down a thought. This whole deal might make a good blues song."

"Like about selling your soul to the devil to be a blues giant? Robert Johnson already did that."

"Some things never go out of style," I said.

"Pain and confusion," Ashton said.

"Love and frustration," I said.

"The blues is just a good man feeling bad." We both laughed.

"Well, the thing is that at least I get to make a record. And if I make it the best I can possibly do, then maybe the music is the way out from under all of this. He can't own me forever."

"You get to be some big music hot shot, you might be able to buy him off."

"You think?"

"Ain't no percentage in thinking, brother. It's not a poor man's game," Ashton said.

"Good lyric," I said. "Who wrote that?"

"I did," he said and grinned.

It made me feel better.

# TEN

I TOLD HARDY TO GO BIG ON A ROAN MARE called Dizzy Flash. She came in at seventeen to one. A few days later I found a real sleeper in the third because it was raining buckets and the gelding really loved to run in the slop. There were no signs in actual races to show that, but I found great times in his workouts while the track was poor. He went off at sixty to one, and Hardy was over the moon at the results. Then, after a ten-day dry spell, I found him a last gasper. That's a horse that's almost ready for the pasture but has one last great race in him. He'd always been a come-from-behind thriller. I remembered him from his younger days and how exciting it had always been to watch him come flying from the back of the pack. Now, though, Falmouth Circuit was old. He hadn't won a race in a long, long time. He was in a race against inexperienced young-sters who had only won one or two races by the time they were four. He was listed as a forty-to-one shot.

The day dawned bright and sunny. Hardy wanted to make an event out of it and arranged to pick me up and take me to the track with him. They picked me up at noon, and we drove to the track. It was crowded, and there was a buzz you could feel in the air. The crowd was alive with it, and the tote board for the second race reflected their excitement. The odds changed every minute as bettors laid down their money on five favorites. Each of them got bet down low. Falmouth Circuit sat unchanged at forty to one for a long time. Hardy kept his eyes on me. I could feel him watching me.

"We gonna do this thing?" he asked finally. There was a rumble of anger in his voice.

"Wait," was all I said.

"Wait for what? You brought me here to play the odds and he's there. He's been there all friggin' day."

"Wait," I said again.

Hardy fumed. Jerry and Vic shrugged their huge shoulders at the same time and rocked on the balls of their feet. We were standing in the throng and leaning on the rail as I watched the tote board, and I could tell that Hardy didn't like being so visible. It was the first hint I got of him being rattled. It was three minutes to post time when the board flickered and the numbers changed. Falmouth Circuit shot up to fifty-five to one.

"Now," I said and turned and headed for the window. The three gangsters fell in behind me. We got our bets down just as the horses were at the gate.

We walked quickly up the stairs to the second balcony, where we could watch the action in the backstretch. The field had already made the first turn and were bunched tightly coming onto the straight. Our horse lagged a good ten lengths behind. The whole grandstand was in a tizzy. The favorites raced shoulder-to-shoulder, and the pace was wild. When they plunged into the third turn, Falmouth Circuit was eight lengths behind. Hardy gave me a hard look. I shrugged. He glowered.

Then the magic happened. It was like the horse found an entirely new set of gears. He closed the gap on the last horse in the pack by the middle of the turn. He was flying. Then he exploded to the outside and began passing horses like they were standing still. The announcer screamed out, "Falmouth Circuit makes a strong bid on the outside." The crowd went nuts.

He caught up to the lead horses five yards into the homestretch. There were four of them spread out in a tight row across the track. Neither gained an inch. Hardy was slamming his rolled-up form against the railing. His face was red with excitement. Everyone was in a frenzy. Time slowed to a heartbeat. The horses closed on the finish line. There was no leader. It looked like it was going to be a photo finish. Then, with scant yards to go, Falmouth Circuit kicked it up another notch. He leaped ahead by a yard, held it and flashed across the line with a narrow victory. There was bedlam around us. Hardy was leaping up and down, hugging me and punching at Jerry and Vic, who had made bets of their own.

Hardy won over fifteen thousand dollars.

"Damn, that was fun," he said on the way out of the grandstand. "Fun to watch and a lot more fun to win. But I gotta admit, you had me worried when you made me wait so long, Cree."

"I just wanted the best numbers for you."

"Well, we got that." He walked ahead of us toward the car and pulled his cell phone out of his pocket. He talked into it as he walked.

"Seems happy," I said to the goons.

"You'd be happy too if you'd loosened a noose," Vic said.

"What do you mean?"

"He owes a bunch to Solly Dario." Jerry elbowed Vic hard in the ribs, and the big man flinched and gave him a hard look. Jerry gave him a harder one back, and Vic put his head down and walked silently. Jerry gave me the same look of stone, and I shut up. But as I watched Hardy talk on the phone, he'd lost the excitement he'd had after the win. He spoke in low tones, grave, and I could sense his seriousness. He was giving deference. He was reporting. Whoever Solly Dario was, he clearly had Hardy's utmost attention. When he closed the phone, he stepped into the car without looking at us and patted his chest pocket where the counter check was. I felt on the verge of a great discovery.

# ELEVEN

ASHTON WAS A WHIZ WITH THE INTERNET. He wasn't much for games or the whole chat thing, but he could find any information that he wanted. His setup was amazing. He had three monitors hooked up to a system that was blazing fast. He showed me the community of info nerds that he belonged to. He searched out everything from the mating habits of the red kangaroo to the latest developments with the space telescope while I sat and watched. Then he typed in *Solly Dario*.

Dario was a street punk who'd worked his way up the criminal ladder with the Ricci crime family. He sat as one of their top lieutenants and also ran his own show. He'd been arrested a number of times but none of the charges had stuck. Somehow key witnesses either changed their minds about their testimony or just failed to show up for court. In his younger days, Dario had been mean and violent and fearless. Now he lived on a big country estate where he raised champion wolfhounds and was a patron of the arts who sponsored museums and libraries. He even had a foundation that awarded bursaries for inner-city kids to go to college.

But he still had his hand in the game. Ashton found references to ongoing investigations with a number of agencies focused on Dario's influence in boxing and a handful of Las Vegas casinos. He was slippery. No one had been able to pin him down on anything, and he lived unthreatened by the law. He was something of a criminal legend.

When he cross-referenced Dario with Winslow Hardy, we found an association that went back a long time. They'd been street kids together. Dario had been the one who brought Hardy to Leo Scalia. While Scalia's ventures never gained the prominence that Dario's did, the two families worked closely with the Ricci organization. And Hardy carried a lot of weight. But his weakness was that he loved to gamble. Ashton found references to a big loss in a Ricci casino that Dario had covered for him.

"That's what Vic meant," I said. "Hardy owes Dario for bailing him out of a mess with the Ricci family. That's why he wanted me in his grips so bad."

"You're the closest thing to a sure thing he's ever found," Ashton said. "Every winner that pays off for him means he can slip the bucks to Dario and take the pressure off. He needs to keep winning."

We looked at each other silently.

"You know what this means then?" I said finally.

"Yeah," Ashton said. "You get him out of debt with Dario, you might be able to walk."

"It means that I just have to keep on winning too."

"You know the odds are against that?"

"It's the only game in town, Ash."

"It's no game when you absolutely have to win."

"That old devil drives a hard bargain," I said.

"Always has," Ashton said. "Always will."

I FOUND BLACKBERRY RAMBLE by accident. I was studying another horse that had caught my interest and began to notice his name regularly in the same lines. He seemed to never be able to get beyond fourth. Judging by what the line said, he ran good races in good company but had never been able to win. "Always a bridesmaid, never a bride" was the line that best described this horse. Until now. The horse that caught my interest was called Upton, and he was a stalker. That meant that he laid off the pace in about fourth position until the homestretch and then outran horses at the very last. Blackberry Ramble ran the same kind of race. What tipped me off was the speed. The two favorites in the race liked to run wire to wire. They were pure speedsters. But this race was longer than they generally ran. It meant that stalkers like Blackberry Ramble could tuck in and let them run and then knock them off in the stretch run more easily. With the presence of Upton in the same race, it meant that my horse would likely go off at really good odds. It wasn't a sure thing, but it certainly was intriguing.

I watched Hardy's eyes light up when I told him. "Likely twenty to one by post time, you figure?" he asked.

"Yeah. Not much more."

"I'll take that any day of the week, hands down," he said.

He went in hard.


THERE ARE MOMENTS in your life that come to define you. Most times you don't even know that's what they are. They're just moments. Just living. Just what you normally do. It's only later when you look back that you discover how big they were. That's what Blackberry Ramble and the eighth race were that day. Everything stayed the same and his numbers sat right where they were supposed to. But something told me to stay off. I didn't risk any of my own money. I didn't say a thing to Hardy. He put his money down like I'd advised. But I couldn't shake the queasy feeling in my gut. I stayed away from the track that day too. Maybe I'd grown a sixth sense. I don't know. All I know is that I didn't feel right, and I laid off. As I walked around that afternoon, the feeling of disaster kept churning in my mind.

Blackberry Ramble stumbled coming out of the gate. It took him precious long seconds to recover and get back into stride. By that time he was at the far outside of the track, and the field was charging through the first turn. He never got back into it. Didn't even come close.

The cell phone went off in my pocket. Hardy told me what happened. "It's what you can never predict," I said.

"Yeah? How much did you lose?" he asked. I could hear the rage in him.

"I didn't lay out a bet," I said.

"Oh yeah? Why's that? It was your pick."

"Gut feeling," I said.

There was a long silence. I waited. I could hear him breathing.

"We need to talk," he said. "I'm picking you up at your place. Be there."

I walked home with slow heavy steps.

# TWELVE

THE BEATING I TOOK WAS VICIOUS. I DIDN'T even know it was coming because Hardy didn't say a word. They picked me up, and as soon as I sat in the backseat, Vic slammed a fist into the back of my head and I crumpled forward. I felt Jerry punch me three times in the ribs before the breath went out of me. Then Vic's big fist crashed into the back of my head again, and I blacked out.

When I came to, I was in a chair at the back of the loading dock at Hardy's warehouse. He pulled on a pair of light boxing gloves, lifted my chin with one hand and smashed a punch into my jaw with the other. Then, as Vic and Jerry held me up, he hammered me in the torso time and time again. The scariest part was the silence. None of them spoke. Hardy kept hitting me, rearing back and punching, and his face didn't change at all. It just stayed cold and hard and bitter. He beat me like a boxer beats a heavy bag. His eyes were dark pits that gave off no light. When he tired, he just waved his hand at the goons, and they let me slump back into the chair.

Hardy leaned against the wall, breathing hard through his mouth. He looked at me through the top of his eyes and sneered. "You cost me ten grand, you useless punk."

The room was spinning. I tried to open my mouth to speak, but it was full of blood. I spit it out at the floor. "Sorry" was all I could get out.

"Sorry? You leave me to carry a bad bet and all you can say is you're sorry?"

"Wasn't a bad bet. Was a good horse."

"So why did you stay out?"

"I don't know. Gut feeling, like I said."

He walked over and pushed my head back with one hand and slammed the other into my belly.

"How's that for a gut feeling, you piece of crap! Give me his hand."

Jerry lifted up my left hand and held it out. Hardy peeled the gloves off and grabbed my first two fingers and bent them back as far as they would go. He leaned forward and glared into my eyes and pushed them back farther and farther. I could feel the tendons stretch, and the pain was incredible.

"I got a gut feeling about you now too, Cree," he said. "I got a feeling maybe a one-handed blues player ain't ever gonna amount to much."

"I didn't know," I gasped.

"You knew enough to stay out without telling me. You knew enough to look out for yourself. You're a player too, Cree. You read it, but you didn't let me know. You let me take a friggin' fall. Big-time."

"I made you money."

He laughed. It was harsh and bitter-sounding. "You made me squat! You're nickel-and-diming me to nowhere. The big money I want? You ain't coming close to getting that, Wonderboy."

"I said I was sorry."

"Oh, believe me, my friend. You haven't even started being sorry."

"What do you mean?"

"What do I mean? What do I mean? I mean I friggin' own you! You, your family, your friends. I friggin' own them too. You cause me to lose, you cause them to lose. Are you getting me now, Cree? Are you?"

I leaned back in the chair and let my arms slump down. "No one else had anything to do with this."

"When you came in, they all came in. That's how it goes, schmuck."

"So what are you gonna do? None of them has any money."

"They can all feel pain."

"They're not responsible for this."

"You're responsible. Call it whatever. Guilt by association if you want."

"So what is it you want me to do?"

"I want my ten grand back. Plus I want what I should have won. You put me in a big hole here, Cree. I need out of it. Fast."

"I can't conjure up a win for you," I said and immediately regretted it.

He knelt down in front of me and looked straight into my eyes. It was his utter stillness that scared me now. I'd never seen someone stay so still, so silent, so threatening without having to move a muscle.

"You'd better. You'd better get to work and pull a friggin' rabbit out of the hat, or people are gonna start to bleed. I promise you that. You got one week."

"One week? For what, twenty thousand or so?"

"Or so," Hardy said. "Call it the upper end, closer to thirty. And that's just for starters."

"I can't do that."

"You can. And you will."

"If I can't?"

He smiled, but it was more like just pulling skin up over his teeth. There was no humor in it, no feeling. It was eerie. Haunting. Disturbing. He reached up and gripped my jaw with one hand. "If you can't, things are really going to go downhill. I don't have the time or the need to carry a bum who doesn't get me what I need. One week, Cree. One week."

He stood up and walked away. Vic and Jerry scowled at me and walked away shaking their heads. The pain I felt all through my body was nothing compared to the sheer terror I felt grip at my belly. It was a long time before I could move.

# THIRTEEN

THEY SAY REVENGE IS A DISH BEST SERVED cold. I never really got that, but I do know that I never took pain very well at all. My father was a strict church-going man. He had no problem with bringing out the strap whenever any of us kids would get out of line. There was always a lecture on how much we had failed him and his god. Then we were walloped, and walloped good. I remember walking away from each of those encounters with his anger and his strap feeling hot, like my skin was burning. It would take me forever to calm down. I think the reason I took to guitar and the blues so eagerly was because it gave me a place to vent. I would slam power chords. I would wrestle notes off the fret board. I would tear through twelve bars. The white-hot heat of my anger fueled my music. Without it, I wonder how much more trouble I might have gotten into. But the pain I felt from Hardy's beating had no such easy outlet.

I churned for days. While my face healed and the stiffness in my ribs and belly eased off, I felt that huge heat I'd felt as a kid. I was hip to the fact that he was too big and bad and mean for me to ever imagine taking him on physically. Plus there were Vic and Jerry to consider. So I focused my thoughts on how I could hurt him as much as he'd hurt me. I felt a bitter taste in my mouth. I felt tears burning at the back of my eyes, and I walked around my room with my fists clenched so hard my forearms ached.

There didn't seem to be any answer for my need for revenge. There didn't seem to be any easy answer for how to get out of his hold either. But I wanted both of those things more than I'd wanted anything. At that point it didn't matter to me if I lost out on the studio and his big promises of a video and connection to music biz movers and shakers. What mattered was that I got free of him. I was bluesman enough to resent the idea of being any man's slave. Finding a way out became my prime focus.

IT CAME TO me as all the best things do—unexpectedly and without stress. It just sort of fell from the sky like a great song lyric does or a fragment of melody that you hum and know in your gut that it's awesome and right. When it came to me. I sat up straight in my chair. It was a simple enough idea, but there were a ton of things that could go wrong. Still, it felt good knowing there was a road to take.

"Play both ends against the middle," I told Ashton.

"I don't get it," he said. "What does that mean exactly?"

I smiled. "It's a player's trick," I said.

"Okay. But I still don't know what it means."

"It means you put out risk on purpose to get your needs met. Like when you want a certain thing to happen, you play the win side and the lose side together so that they cancel each other out and you get the result you want anyway."

"So you put your head in the noose and hope no one kicks the chair out from under your feet?"

"Sounds about right."

"In terms of Hardy, though, what do you mean?"

"I mean I play him for the money, not the horse."

"Is this some kind of Indian thing, Cree? Because I'm really not following you at all."

I laughed, and he looked worried. We ordered ourselves another round of coffees, and after they arrived, I leaned close to him and told him the details as they had come to me. It was complicated and took a long time. When I finished, he sat back in his chair and stared out the window. Then he looked at me and nodded. But he looked a hell of a lot more worried.

# FOURTEEN

WE USED ASHTON'S COMPUTER. WHEN I
found horses that interested me, we researched them. In a
few days we learned more about bloodlines, breeding, sires,
dams, thoroughbred farms, the structure of racetracks,
horse anatomy, how they run and the science of racing
horses than I ever thought I'd know before. Everything
I knew had come from firsthand experience. But the tech-
nology gave me a university degree in understanding the
math and the science behind it all. When it came to plotting
odds, it sure helped. My head felt stuffed with information.

Hardy only called once.

"Time's getting short, Cree."

"I know," I said. "I'm just making sure I put you onto a sure thing."

"You'd better." He'd hung up abruptly, and Ashton gave me that grave, worried look again.

I knew that a good horse could run anywhere from eight to twelve times a season. At smaller tracks like the one we had in town, they might go more often, so we narrowed our search to include only those who looked like their owners were priming them for a climb up the ladder to major tracks. It meant they ran fewer races, but they were better contests. We also focused on horses that worked out very well and steadily but had no wins in races against good competition. We wanted speed. We wanted endurance. We wanted a late move in the final stages in the race. It meant that we wanted a router. In track talk, a router is a horse that runs routes or races of a mile or more. The sprints, those short races where blinding speed separates winners from losers, are harder to gauge and play. But routers give you more laps, more time and more room to gather information on their past efforts. So we narrowed our search to longer races and the routers that ran them.

It was important that we have a longer race to play. It was vital that we had as much information on the field of horses that would run the race we chose. It was also critical that we knew the layout of the track as closely as possible. On smaller tracks like the one we went to, the turns are sharper. It means horses on the outside aren't as far off the lead as it looks from the grandstand. It also means front-runners, horses who use their speed to get out fast and try to hold it, are less likely to put up a huge lead because they have to negotiate the turns with more care.

Ashton showed me how to research all of it. I admired him for his computer knowledge. He was impressed with my inside scoop on racing. Together we put together a "book," a list of horses with numbers we liked and that fit our preferences. In the end we whittled it down to three. When we compared the numbers, we liked our list. Then we checked the racing schedule of each of them and found that one had been raced hard very recently, and we cut our list to two. Then we headed for the track.

A horse by the numbers is just a shadow. You have to get out in the stink of the barn and the backtrack where they live and work to really see them. I had enough connections left from my days as an exercise groom to get back there with no problem. It was an awesome world. The barns were long and low and cool. They were filled with impressive animals. When you're in the stands or watching on TV, you never really get a sense of how big and powerful a thoroughbred horse really is. To get the full-meal deal on that, you have to stand next to one. You have to touch one and feel the ripple of muscle under your palm, hear the breath huffed out like a bellows and hear the stamp of one hoof that clumps like a ton of cement on the straw bed of their stalls. You know then how powerful they are. When they look at you with those huge bottomless shining eyes, you get a feel for how smart they are, how much they know about you just from looking at you.

"Wow," Ashton said. "These guys are enormous."

"When you stand near the starting gate and they all fire off at the same time, it's like the ground explodes," I said.

"I want to do that."

"We will. As soon as we finish here."

The horse we'd come to see was named Deb's Wild Fancy. He was a big, rangy-looking chestnut gelding. When we found him, he was being led to the track for a workout.

He pranced. The groom leading him was laughing as Deb's Wild Fancy literally danced sideways and then back the other way as though he were in a choreographed dance routine. He had a lot of energy. The groom turned him over to the exercise rider and came and leaned on the rail beside us. His name was Ralph, and he was eager to talk. He told us the gelding would run in three days in a mile-and-a-half race to earn a step up the ladder. The field had been chosen for him. A pack of good strong horses with good reputations, but whose finishes lacked the burst that Deb's Wild Fancy had. He was placed to win. Then he was being transported to a senior track in California where he'd run against some of the best two- and three-year-olds in the country. It was everything we wanted to hear.

Then we saw him run. It was like watching ribbon unfold time after time. He was so smooth, it looked effort-less. The rider held him back with two hands. Breezing, it's called. Then, just as they passed us, the rider dropped his hands an inch with the reins, and Deb's Wild Fancy became everything the computer numbers said he was: a charging, relentless ground-eater with speed to spare. And my ticket out.

# FIFTEEN

"SO WE HAVE THE HORSE. WHAT DO WE DO now?" Ashton asked. "There's no way we can influence what the odds on him will be."

"True enough," I said, looking out the window at the street from our favorite table in the coffee joint. "But we won't mess with his odds. We mess with the others."

"What do you mean?"

"I mean the form comes out the day before. Everyone who's a serious player gets it as soon as it hits the street. The line on Deb's Wild Fancy is going to show his lack of wins and fades at the finish going into a race with proven horses. He's an underdog."

"Yeah. So?"

"So we let him stay that way. Our job is to influence the other numbers and keep action off our ride."

"How do we do that?"

"Hardy," I said.

"Hardy? How is he going to help us?" Ashton looked worried, and I grinned. I was starting to get a plan on the rails. It felt good to be in the game again.

"We don't tell him that he is," I said.

"Oh, that's just great!" Ashton said, slapping the table with his palm. "The last time you didn't tell him about something almost got you killed."

"Yes. But he showed me something. Something that we needed to know."

"And what might that be?"

"Desperation," I said. "He wasn't angry that I didn't keep him in the play. He was hot because he lost—and he can't afford to lose."

"So?"

"So we put him on a different horse."

He gave me a look of utter disbelief.

"You want to get him to put money down on a horse that you know isn't going to do anything? How is that going to help?"

"When there's a sudden drop of loot, it shows on the odds board right away. The amount in the win pool goes up, and the odds go down. Every player worth his salt watches how the pool is being affected. It tells them where the action is."

He thought for a moment.

"So you get Hardy to lay down a bundle on this other horse. That makes the players react and the odds change. So the numbers on our horse go up?"

"You're a born handicapper, kid." I grinned.

"I just want to live to see thirty," he said. "Hanging with you sometimes makes that feel like a challenge."

"Yeah, well, it's all about the road and not the map, baby."

"Cool enough," he said and clapped me on the shoulder. "But maybe we can try truckin' down something other than a dirt road sometime there, Lightnin'." He laughed. I felt good. Ashton was a great friend.

THE THING ABOUT horse players is that the smarter they get, the less they really know. Numbers are like a complicated chord progression. You can stare at them all you like, but you actually have to put your hand on the guitar to make any sense of it. Horse players sit back and watch numbers and never do anything to work with them. They come to believe that the numbers have a mind of their own and will fall into the pattern they're supposed to, and that their job is to watch them and react when all the signs are clear. This is what I was counting on.

The other thing that I was counting on is what players dread the most. The unseen. The weird little things that go on in the background that affect the way things turn out. A bandage or a tape job on a fetlock or a knee. A sheen of liniment on the shoulder or the haunch. Blinkers over the eyes or tape on the ears. Or just the sudden appearance of numbers in a cold hard splash that drives them to the windows in droves. Horse players are a superstitious bunch. They're certain that the Fates are lined up to pick their pockets, and the things they can't control or understand send them into hard mental tailspins. I needed that to happen. I needed Hardy for that.

The other thing I needed was money to play. A lot of it. When the big moment came, I needed to be at the window with a pailful. I knew the only place I could turn for that. But the thing I needed most desperately was one of those things I couldn't control. I could get Hardy to believe he was riding the next sure thing. I could have a plan for play money. What I couldn't control was the weather the day of the race, a sudden accident in the exercise ring, a horse in the field juiced on speed, a spill during the race, an injury or the sudden pulling of my horse at the gate. There were more than enough imagined pitfalls. I could only take care of the things I could control. I left Ashton at the coffee joint and went to do just that.

# SIXTEEN

RACE DAY DAWNED LIKE A MINOR MIRACLE.
There wasn't a cloud in the sky and not even a hint of a
breeze. It was warm. The whole day smelled like roses. If
there were such a thing as an omen, then I guess the day
breaking open like that was it for me. I called Ashton, and
we arranged to meet at the coffee shop and then go for
breakfast. I showered and headed out. But Vic and Jerry
were waiting for me on the porch. They stood there mute
as statues. I couldn't see their eyes behind their mirrored
shades. All Vic did was extend an arm and indicate that
I should walk ahead of them to the limo that sat at the

curb, its tinted windows giving no hint as to who was inside. Jerry reached around me and opened the back door. I looked inside. Hardy was sitting there with Ashton, who looked pale and very nervous.

"What's this?" I asked.

"Insurance," Hardy said and smiled.

"Against what?"

"Me gettin' the friggin' blues, Cree."

"I got you on a good horse."

"That's what buddy boy is here to ensure. The boys will sit on him until we see what goes down."

"I'm telling you what's going to go down is that you're walking away with a ton of cash today."

He laughed. It was a cold laugh, empty of any feeling. It sent a chill down my spine.

"Words. That's all that is. Words. Until I see something concrete, your buddy the nerd gets babysat. If the outcome is good, the outcome is good. If it isn't...well, use your imagination. What's this magic horse's name anyway?"

"Regal Splendor. He's a six-to-one shot in the second."

"You want me to go big on a six-to-one shot?"

"No. I want you in on the next sure thing. It's what you asked."

"Regal Splendor. Sounds like...whattaya call it...a good sign."

"It is."

I looked at Ashton. He shrugged and looked at the floor. Jerry put a big wide hand in the middle of my back and pushed me into the car. I sat on the jump seat facing Hardy. He sat back and smoothed his clothes and grinned humorlessly. We pulled into traffic. Vic and Jerry eased in behind us in the SUV. I coughed nervously, and Hardy's cold stare froze me to the seat. He eased his jacket back and showed me the butt of an automatic pistol. Then he closed it and patted the small bulge where it sat in the holster under his armpit.

"Ah, a day at the races. So stylish. So fun. Don't you think, there, nerd?"

He jostled Ashton in the ribs with his elbow. My friend just continued to stare at the floor. We drove to the track in silence. Hardy leaned back in the seat staring at me, eyes as empty as any I had ever seen. Just at that moment, the plan I had concocted offered me little comfort.

WE KILLED TIME until the races started by cruising through the barns. Hardy was his most charming self. He scored a lot of points with handlers and grooms with his jokes and the roll of bills he showed buying coffees for them all. When he asked a few people about how Regal Splendor looked, he got nothing but strong opinions about his chances. A long shot, but a horse that would definitely be in the race even if it was the favorites that would rule the day. He seemed pleased with that.

"Did your homework," he said to me as we walked back to the grandstand.

"It's what you asked," I said.

"How long do I wait before I put the bet down?"

"I'd wait until the end of the first race." Deb's Wild Fancy was in the second too. "Don't want to go too soon and tip your hand. But you also don't want to wait too long either," I said.

"Are you in on this one this time?"

"You bet," I said, and he grinned.

HARDY WON FIFTEEN HUNDRED dollars in the first race on a horse I picked out of the post parade. She just looked good. He came back from the window with a gleam in his eye.

"If that's how this is going to go today, you and the nerd will be doing whatever it is nerds do at night."

I only nodded. The numbers on the tote board read exactly as I wanted them to. Regal Splendor moved up to eight to one, and there wasn't a move on Deb's Wild Fancy at all. He stayed at thirty to one. Hardy watched me read the board. I could feel his tension rising. When the numbers flashed across in an update with twelve minutes to go, I saw that they had stayed the same. "Time to go," I said.

"Everything good?"

"Everything's perfect." I stood and followed him to the window. I was counting on long lines that would let me slip into a separate one from Hardy. My luck held. He only glanced at me. I shrugged and pointed to the number of people ahead of him. He nodded. I waited for him by the stairs. He had the assured glow that bettors have when they know they're on a sure thing. He was actually smiling. He clapped me soundly on the back, and we walked back to our seats. The crowd was buzzing. There were three horses bet down to almost identical odds. Then, thirty seconds before post time, the numbers flashed in the final update and Regal Splendor sat at ten to one. Hardy's smile got even bigger.

"How big did you go?" I asked.

"I went ten large."

"Nice payout." I said.

"It will be," he said. Then he looked at me sternly. "Won't it, Cree?"

"I told you, there's a ton of cash to be won on this race."

The track announcer said the fateful words, "And they're at the post." The crowd hushed, and I could feel the pulse of adrenaline everywhere. Hardy's legs bumped up and down, and his hands tapped the top of his thighs. The gate flew open and they were off.

# SEVENTEEN

IT WENT JUST AS I THOUGHT IT WOULD. THE
three favorites controlled the race. They went to the front
and challenged the rest of the field to stay with them. Regal
Splendor ran fourth with a two-length gap between him
and the favorites. Deb's Wild Fancy hung back in seventh
position and ran evenly without attracting any notice
from either the crowd or the other jockeys. The pace was
frantic. There wasn't a nose between the three leaders, and
the crowd was wild. Regal Splendor made a small move
coming into the final turn and moved just behind them.
Hardy jumped up and down in place beside me. I couldn't

hear myself think for the noise all around us. There'd been plenty of money bet, and people were going crazy.

Then, as they rounded the turn into the homestretch, Deb's Wild Fancy came charging out of nowhere. He blasted into the straight. Regal Splendor had moved into a small lead, but the leaders were still in a tight pack. Deb's Wild Fancy had to run wide, but he had a ton of gas left and his stride stretched out. He galloped hard to pull even as the crowd noise became enormous. Then it was between him and Regal Splendor. I don't think I breathed. Hardy was bashing me on the shoulder and his face was crazed and wild and he yelled things that didn't even sound like words to me. Then with ten yards to go, Deb's Wild Fancy eased ahead and won going away by three-quarters of a length. Hardy slumped down into his seat. The crowd was electrified by the race, and the hubbub was tremendous. I sat down quietly beside Hardy.

"Let me see your ticket," he said.

I handed it to him. He looked at it briefly. He nodded. He scowled. Then he tucked it into his pocket and elbowed me hard to my feet and put his hand inside his jacket. "Walk," was all he said.

He walked behind me all the way to the parking lot. He didn't say a word to me, but he didn't have to. The same unnerving quiet that had settled over him during my beating spoke volumes to me as we walked. Some people carry the threat of themselves like a cloud, and Hardy's roiled all around me. When we got to the car, he raised his hand and Vic and Jerry pulled up the black Navigator with Ashton inside.

"What's to it, boss?" Vic asked.

"He played me," Hardy said. "We'll settle up at the warehouse."

Jerry got out of the Navigator and grabbed me by the elbow. Hard. Then he pushed me into the backseat, and I slammed into Ashton with such force that our heads banged together. Vic drove fast following Hardy, and neither of them spoke. Ashton and I could only glance at each other, but I could tell that he was worried. I was beyond that. The ticket Hardy grabbed from me had been a thousand-dollar ticket. It was a big win. But it wasn't going to be enough.

Vic and Jerry manhandled us through the loading dock and into the warehouse. Hardy had gotten there moments before. There were no employees left in the building. It was deathly quiet. While Vic stood in front of us, Jerry placed a pair of chairs in the middle of the floor on a large sheet of heavy plastic.

"What's that for?" Ashton asked.

"Makes cleanup easier," Vic said and grinned.

"Cleanup of what?" he asked.

"You," Vic said.

Hardy came down the stairs from his office. He'd changed into a jogging suit and black leather gloves. He was carrying a hammer and a chisel. He walked past his henchmen without a word and separated the chairs so that they sat facing each other. Then he motioned for Vic and Jerry to bring us over. They shoved us so hard that we stumbled and crashed into each other, and Ashton sprawled on the plastic. Vic kicked him and hauled him to his feet. Jerry slapped me on the back of the head and I fell into a chair, nearly tipping over before I planted my feet and settled. Hardy stood in front of us tapping the head of the hammer on the chisel.

"Do you know what you cost me, Cree?" he asked.

"Ten large?" I asked.

"More than that, buddy boy. I needed this race. I needed the win. You have no idea how badly."

"Actually, I do." I said.

"You do?"

"Yeah. Your goons let it slip that you owe a lot of money to Solly Dario."

He flashed a look at Vic and Jerry, who shrugged and looked away. I could see him grip the tools tighter in his fist. "Yeah, well, none of that matters now. What matters is that you played me. You took my trust and my ten grand and set me back. Again. Bigger. With more consequences. And I got to even up now."

He stepped up to Ashton, and Vic moved in to press him into his seat by pushing down on his shoulders. Hardy knelt and held the edge of the chisel just below his kneecap. "You ever seen a sculpture being made, Cree?"

"No," I said, barely above a whisper.

"Messy. Bits of stuff flying all over. But before I start, I just want to ask you one question."

"What's that?" I asked.

"Who fronted you the grand to lay down on the horse?"

"I did." The voice came from the door of the loading dock, and the three gangsters spun around to see who spoke.

"Solly," Hardy said. The tools dropped onto the plastic.

Solly Dario and four of his men strode into the warehouse. They were all business. Vic and Jerry stepped back away from us. Solly stepped up to Hardy and stood mere inches away, staring at him sternly. "Come to collect," he said.

"I ain't got it, Solly. I woulda. But the kid played me."

"Oh, I'm not here to collect from you, Winslow. I'm here to collect from Cree."

Hardy looked at me and just stared with his mouth hanging wide open.

# EIGHTEEN

"YOU GOT A GOOD KID HERE, WINSLOW. BE A shame to see you put him out of commission." Solly began peeling off his gloves finger by finger and eyeing Hardy all the while. Ashton and I watched and waited.

"He don't play straight, Solly," Hardy said. "He's got no code."

"Fact is, he does."

"Whattaya mean?"

Dario finished removing his gloves, folded them gently and laid them in the pocket of his overcoat.

"He's got a code and he's got moxie. He come to me.

Told my boys you sent him, and he told me about your issue."

"My issue?" Hardy put a hand against his chest and bowed slightly.

"You gave the kid a week to come up with the juice you still owe me. That's a big load to throw off on a young kid. Especially one who has such a good high end as this kid does."

"Solly, I was just taking care of your end."

"My end takes care of itself, Winslow. Always has, always will. Like this kid walkin' through my door. Good things just come to me." Solly looked at them, and his four boys all grinned. "So he tells me about his gig with you. Then he tells me how he needs a hand to get this done. So I listen like any good businessman would. Turns out he wants to teach you something, and me, I figure that's a good thing on accounta you being into me for so much means you could use a lesson in how things work."

"I don't get it," Hardy said.

Dario patted him on the cheek.

"I know you don't. The kid needed someone to front the cash for a big roll out on this horse. Said if I did, he would earn me back the vig and the juice from you and a whole lot more."

"I still don't get it," Hardy said.

"And that's why you'll never be a good businessman, Winslow. See, the kid knew the horse would win, but he needed someone to take the attention off him at the last minute. Hence your ten large.

"You dumped this big wager, and it shows up in the win pool. That gets every player in the joint drooling, and they lay out more and no one touches the money horse. In fact, his odds go up. When that happens, I lay down my wager at the very last minute, and next thing you know, I'm collecting big. Big. And the thing is, the kid would only do it if your debt was cleared with the winnings."

"He still played me for the sap," Hardy said.

"Get over yourself, Winslow. The kid knew you could handle the ten grand. You were only sweating what you owed me. You were the means to the end, and if he played you, he did it perfectly. Perfectly. Kinda like he plays the blues."

"You heard him?"

"Naturally. I said he had a good high end. Kid's gonna make a big splash, and I'm in the front door."

"So I owe you nothing?"

"That's right. Free and clear. Just like the kid and his pal here."

"But he still belongs to me, right? He still plays the track for me?"

"Winslow, you don't hear so good sometimes. I said free and clear. Along with clearing your debt, he cleared himself too. That means his family, all the connections to him you got too. Granted, every now and then he's going to do me a favor when a sure thing comes up, and maybe I'll let you in on that action when it happens. Then again, maybe I won't."

"So what's the lesson I'm supposed to learn here?" Hardy asked. He looked beat.

"Tell him, Cree." Dario grinned.

Hardy looked at me. "There is only ever really one sure thing," I said.

"Oh, yeah," Hardy said coldly. "And what might that be?"

"You have to make your own luck, because there's never really a next sure thing."

"Still talking in song lyrics, aren't you?" Hardy asked.

As it turned out, I was.

# EPILOGUE

WE FINISHED RECORDING MY FIRST ALBUM within a month. It was called *Sure Thing Blues*, and the critics hailed it for the force of its guitar work and its intelligent lyrics. By the end of that summer, it was the number-one blues recording in the country and I had three prime videos and a major concert tour opening for Buddy Guy. Ashton became my manager. He put together one of the hottest bands on the planet to back me up, and we worked the crowds like rock and rollers. We were a hit. My father came to one of our gigs. When he came to the dressing room after, there were tears in his eyes.

"I never knew," he said.

"Never knew what, Dad?" I asked.

He grabbed me into the first real big hug I remember getting from him and held me tight for a long time. "Never knew the many ways we can be blessed. You've been blessed with incredible music, and I've been blessed with a musician and a son."

We've been real tight ever since.

Hardy faded away, and even though I caught sight of him the few times I ventured to the track, he pretended not to see me. That was fine with me. Solly Dario financed the CD, the video and the equipment, and the buses and the trucks we needed to tour, but was content to be a silent partner. No one ever knew about our connection. Still, when there were good numbers in the racing form I let him know. I don't know if he ever made the bets, and I don't care. What mattered was that I was on my way to becoming the next great bluesman. I settled into the life of writing and playing and chasing my star across the heavens that had opened up for me.

Oh, and what Hardy said about talking in song lyrics? He was right. The first single from my debut album was called "The Next Sure Thing."

*You can make your money in the fields all day,*

*Or you can make your money in a different way,*

*But you gotta get up and show your pluck,*

*Because winners are the ones who make*

*their own kind of luck.*

*There's winners and there's losers, and*

*here's the thing:*

*You can waste a lot of time waitin' on the*

*next sure thing.*

WAUBGESHIG RICE is an author and journalist from Wasauksing First Nation on Georgian Bay. He has written three fiction titles, and his short stories and essays have been published in numerous anthologies. His most recent novel, *Moon of the Crusted Snow*, was published in 2018 and became a national bestseller. He graduated from Ryerson University's journalism program in 2002 and spent the bulk of his journalism career at CBC, most recently as host of *Up North*, the afternoon radio program for northern Ontario. He lives in Sudbury with his wife and two sons.

RICHARD WAGAMESE was a Canadian author and journalist. An Ojibwe from the Wabaseemoong Independent Nations in Northwestern Ontario, he published thirteen books in his lifetime and left manuscripts that have led to four books being published posthumously. He was best known for his 2012 novel, *Indian Horse*, which won the Burt Award for First Nations, Métis and Inuit Literature in 2013, won the popular vote in the 2013 edition of CBC's Canada Reads and was adapted into a 2017 feature length film of the same title, released after his death.